THE GOLDEN GOOSE

Ivan Southall

The GOLDEN GOOSE

GREENWILLOW BOOKS, New York

First American Edition

10   9   8   7   6   5   4   3   2   1

Library of Congress Cataloging in Publication Data
Southall, Ivan. The Golden Goose.
Sequel to: King of the sticks.
Summary: Now in the custody of Preacher Tom, who
believes him to have special powers, slow-witted
Custard is forced to search for gold.
[1. Australia—Fiction]
I. Title.   PZ7.S726Go   [Fic]
ISBN 0-688-00608-6   81-2047
                               AACR2

TO ANDREW SOUTHALL

CONTENTS

THE GOLDEN GOOSE

chapter one

THE DESPERATE COUNTRY

MORE THAN a hundred years ago the kid they called Custard trudged behind the small grey horse far out upon the plain. Poor Custard. Poor Little Horse. Each had a few strong words to say about it, in his own way, from time to time.

"I'm going to die," Custard reckoned. "Or I'm dead already and gone to Hell. What do you bet?"

On he trudged, singing songs to himself, so quietly Prospector Tom never heard the words, though the man was much too busy with visions to give attention to matters as trivial as Custard's songs. And sometimes Custard would run like mad to make up the ground he'd lost. Getting left behind out there would be the end.

Well, if you didn't die of hunger or thirst or raving madness, you'd get a spear in your back.

Prospector Tom was out in front, striding on as always, but Custard never wondered whether he was mad or not, for no one that Custard knew was not slightly mad at best, even his mother, and she was far away in the south or the north or the east—wherever home was, wherever.

On he trudged, scared of the wilderness all about, yet waiting for the chance to run for his life, but never seeing a house, or a hut, or a tent, never seeing a white man, never seeing a chance. Nothing walking upright on its own two legs ever crossed his path. All he felt were *presences*. The kind of presences that prickle your hair or flutter at the nerves in your chest.

It was hard being a kid like Custard, having one foot in the real world and the other foot somewhere else, forever stumbling down the middle, not sure what was real, not sure what was not, not sure whether he should scream and scream and scream, "Go away, all you demons and you devils, and let me be myself."

On trudged Custard, listening for the sound of horses, coming fast. Listening for the call to halt, shouted out sternly, shouted out harshly, "Stop, old Tom Button, in the name of Queen Victoria, or we'll shoot you dead as rigor mortis."

But they never came or shouted. They never fired a shot. Prospector Tom never fell flat, gasping, twitching, croaking. The troopers didn't come. And Custard couldn't believe that.

"Why don't they come? Where are they? Where's my brother Seth? Where's my mum?"

Day after day Custard said it. Twenty days. Forty days. Sixty days. Then he stopped counting.

Custard sang a song about Prospector Tom as he went plodding on.

Plod plod
Plod plod,

Mash his tumkin,
Spinning Jenny,
Kill him dead-o,
Kill him stupid.

Plod plod
Plod plod,

Bash his thumbkin
If he's any,
Smash his pumpkin,
One's too many,
Kill him dead-o,
Kill him stupid.

Plod plod
Plod plod,

Thrash his bumkin,
Six a penny,
Hi de duddle
Kill ole Tommy,
Kill him dead-o,
Kill him stupid.

Plod plod
Plod plod.

Not that the song meant much. It didn't have to. Making
it up was the thing. Singing took the strain off things a bit.

There was Prospector Tom, still striding on towards the
dawn of golden promises, always putting on a show, though
no one was there to look that Custard knew about. Still
striding on, like an actor playing someone else's life, playing

it bigger than it was. Shielding his eyes from the sun. Sometimes looking back. But not often. Keeping up with him was Custard's problem.

Six feet four, that old fellow was, with a tall black hat up on top, a very strange sight he was, though you got used to it. Over seven feet tall in all he was—counting in his hat and his boots and the length of him in the middle, an awful lot of man to go chasing up the hills and through the gullies and across the plain, particularly when you'd been kidnapped.

I mean, *kidnapped*, thought Custard.

I mean, *taken away from home and sold into slavery or something*.

Grrrrrr, thought Custard.

And all the days were the same, except that some were hotter than others, and some were blustrier, and some were dustier, and some started earlier, and some ended later, and on some days you cut ten sticks to go dowsing for gold, and on some days you cut three, though one would have done, and every day you ate less than the day before, which was a real terrible situation.

That silly old man didn't even have a gun to shoot the dinner. He'd had one at the start, but threw it away.

"It's evidence," he said. And threw it in the river.

Plop.

So kangaroos hopped along beside, and bush turkeys preened their feathers on every rock, and ducks flew overhead, and everywhere you looked was beautiful, beautiful dinner, except that you couldn't have any of it unless you could catch it from running along behind.

I'll fade away, thought Custard.

One moment there I'll be, looking like Custard, the next there'll be nothing. There'll be a hole in the air, the same size as me.

"Where's Custard?" they'll say.

"Here I am. Look over here! Here I am."

"That's a funny hole in the air," they'll say. "It talks."

"It's not a hole. It's me."

But they'll shake their heads and go away.

"It's awful," sighed Custard, as he went plodding on. "I wish my mum was here. She'd fix him. She'd pull the trigger. Bang. And he'd be the hole in the air instead of me."

Then at about noon every day, round about the high heat of it, the old fellow would head for high ground. For a hillock or a nice rock. And up he'd stand on it, tall and straight, against the sun, lifting up his voice, resonant and rich and as ripe as plums, being Preacher Tom again, as everyone used to call him before he got into the kidnapping business. Well, before his sons forced him into the kidnapping business; the fate of most fathers, as he'd say himself, being to pick up the bits their kids leave lying around; the bits in this case being Custard.

There he'd be, on his rock, holding up an arm like a bishop about to bless the mob, and he'd start rolling his rrr's and making long words. Orating, he called it. "A very important function, boy, what marks the difference between the humans and the beasts."

So he'd start bellowing out across the dusty wastes. "Oh Father God, thus we come to sacred ground. Through privation and suffering at last it is found. I'm given the vision. I see it clear. The Age of Gold begins right here." If the rhyme came out right he might say it again a couple of times.

And perhaps Little Horse would whinny a bit, because it was getting near lunch. And Custard would start thinking of the nice drink of water that should be waiting in the goatskin bag. Then he'd think of the dough that Prospector Tom would be baking in the coals quite soon, and his nostrils would start twitching. Then he'd think about eating it. But Prospector Tom would be going on with his orating.

"Gold is the power by which I change the world I live in. Gold is the power given me by God. Hallelujah. Though I'd respectfully suggest that it's about time we started seeing some of it. By gold I level the mountains and dam the rivers and challenge the rights of Queens and Kings and bring justice to the downtrodden and comfort to the poor and bread to the starving. And one other matter, Father God, I would keep before your attention; leaving enough of this here gold for my personal manipulation, to save my stupid sons from the hangman's rope, to pay the Queen's bullies. And to Thee, Father God, be the glory."

There he'd stand, his ear cocked, squinting out across hills worn smooth, and creek beds baked dry, and plains ever-rolling, and space never-ending, and skies so hazed and so glazed they were almost white with the glare of it. Not that he saw very much of it, Prospector Tom being a sufferer of the middle-aged disease of having eyes not like what they used to be. And the winds would roar in from the west, punching and panting across deserts of sand and deserts of salt and places inconceivable never seen by a white man, that they might come in the end to buffet at him. Then he'd come down from his rock. "God's not listening, boy. He's not hearing me. I wonder about this place. I wonder about this land. I wonder if it's the Devil's Kingdom.

"It's good country for dying in, boy.

"Nothing's going my way, boy.

"Two wrongs don't make a right. I should have taken you home to your mother.

"But a madness comes over a man at the thought of gorgeous gold."

chapter two

THE HULLABALOO

BACK AT the beginning, after they had taken Custard away, the brave Rebecca said, "My poor simple son is dead. Will I ever understand why those hooligans came through my door? To come without warning or sense of any kind and to take him away like a foal or a calf. My poor son. He's not as the rest of us are. They'll learn that soon enough. They'll throw him out to die."

There was a curse upon her, upon the brave Rebecca, and upon the land itself, this cruel and desperate land at the bottom of the earth.

Her beautiful Bella, her one daughter, swinging legs under her that never again would walk without sticks. Her perfect Bella becoming unperfect. Wasn't that enough?

Her good and gorgeous Adam, her beautiful husband, those long years back, coming home from market on the floor of his cart, coming home silent, without his song, without his money, without his life. Leaving Seth, his son, to stand up like a man, to be a man before it was time to stop being a boy. Poor Seth. All he had was work, and a little rum to help him forget.

Adam had crossed the earth to pioneer this place, to make this farm, to build this house, to lie dead and cold and silent in alien yellow earth.

Adam and Rebecca and Seth and Bella—and Custard, a baby at his mother's breast—twelve thousand miles they had come together, under sail, with courage and with hope, across vast oceans, through days and weeks and months and calms and storms, into this harsh land that resembled nothing they had been led to expect.

"This fag-end of the earth."

Rebecca shouted it at the night.

"I will avenge," she vowed. "I'll kill for this. I'll ride to the governor and hammer at his door.

"Sir. I am Rebecca of Inglewood. They have kidnapped my son. I demand a company of soldiers that I may go after him."

Then I'll ride at the head of my soldiers across field and forest and hill until I run them to earth, those murderers who took my boy away in the night, and my deed will not be forgotten until the ages lie down to sleep.

Father God, you gave them authority over me.

They have left me widowed and weeping for my son.

They have destroyed the sweetness of my life.

But they broke only my heart.

I am the Amazon, and they will speak in dread of me.

I will exact an eye for an eye and a tooth for a tooth and a life for a life.

But her spirit passed from the crazy crests into the deep valleys.

"The dead are the dead," said the voices in the valleys,

"and are required to care for each other in their own quiet place. Be calm, Rebecca. It is your duty to care for your brave and beautiful Bella on her sticks, and for your gorgeous Seth, Seth who took up his father's yoke, Seth who has been the man and protected you and done so little for himself.

"How can you go after your son when he lies as dead as the generations that sleep? Somewhere on your journey, somewhere down the years of your searching, you would step across his resting place and see only flowers growing. How could he call you as you passed?"

Rebecca shouted in her grief and cats fled up the chimney and creatures stirred in the forest and Bella and Seth wakened in the house.

"Oh, Mum," Seth called, "the kid's gone, it's done, it's over. I work like an ox. You know I need my sleep."

Bella's voice came also in the dark. "Have a bit of faith, Mum, that someone'll bring him back."

"My husband Adam is dead, all these long years dead. No one brought Adam back and no one brought life to your legs, Bella. And now my helpless son is dead as well."

Callers started coming to the brave Rebecca's door, from round about, from town, and from far off.

They waited until Seth was at market, or somewhere else perhaps. There they'd stand, as they had stood before, when her gorgeous Adam had gone down to the earth and his dust had barely settled. Then they had come because she was a woman of property, and pleasing to look

at, and why should a woman such as she be left to lament?
But they left her to her sorrows soon enough.

The mad woman, they called her, with respect, after
the affair of Harry Kinsella Smith. She shot off his hand,
aiming from the hip.

It was for gold that they came now, to her gate, bailed
up there by White Dog, if White Dog was on the loose.
For gold, men would risk even their necks, though confronting White Dog jowl to jowl was an appalling fright,
and confronting the lady herself was a foolhardy act.

Up she'd come from the house, that fortress house built
by Adam years back, her long black skirts cracking like
sailcloth, in she'd come with her gun.

"Yes?"

And with one word she would convey her anger and
contempt.

The she-tiger, they thought. And some were stammer-
ing by then, wondering if their brains were addled, wondering how anyone could have imagined that she'd share
the secret of her loot, of her lovely gold locked up in that
box of solid oak, studded round with bronze and barred
with bolts, of which they had heard so much in the taverns
and alehouses. And they would make noises of a kind, as
if trying to utter a password that might cause caves to open
or mountains to split.

"Gold," she'd say, with derision. "Preserve me from
fools. My boy wouldn't have known gold from old boots!
Would you know it yourself? I wouldn't know it from a
pain in my back.

"You think I've got a hoard of it under my bed? You think my boy Custard found it by divining with sticks? Would I live in this God-forsaken country if I had gold to pay my way out of it?

" 'Dig here for water,' he used to say. And we'd dig. And we'd find bones. What else is there in this desolation except the dead, except their bones, except heartbreak and sorrow and grief? Find gold where you're lucky to raise a crop of weeds that don't wilt in mid-growth? Gold in this fag-end of the Earth?"

Notices went up: *Trespassers will be shot.*

After that she pulled the trigger as White Dog warned her of a stranger's approach.

An odd creature was White Dog, a large and ugly and savage beast, chained within sight of the house if Seth was at home; but running free if Seth was anywhere else. People called him the Wolf Dog, and in his dark heart he held to a memory of the ones who had come in masks, who had struck him senseless with clubs.

Day by day White Dog remembered. Day by day he waited. Bella knew that, because Bella could feel those things.

Day by day Bella became more and more uneasy in that house.

Four horsemen reined in at the gate. That much Rebecca could see as she came storming out. White Dog was among them and riding whips were cracking and Rebecca shrilled across the gap, "On your way, or else."

Flocks of parrots screeched into flight through the forest trees and every creature in hearing started up in protest or in fright.

"Call your dog off!"

"I shoot to kill," shrilled the brave Rebecca, still striding forth, "if you pass the gate."

"Put your gun down, madam! Call your dog off!"

Back and forth rang the shouts.

"His Excellency, madam, presents his respects."

"The notice is there," shrilled Rebecca, "in clear sight. Pass the gate and your heads come off."

Bella followed on her sticks, swinging on her sticks, almost running on her sticks. "Mum, Mum, Mum. You'll kill someone yet."

At the gate a pistol went at arm's length above men and horses and dog and fired straight up.

"They're soldiers," shouted Bella. "Oh, Mum, can't you see that?"

"I'll soldier them," she shrilled, and fired across the treetops. "Hooligans, I call them, and Seth gone but two hours at that."

"Madam, the governor!"

"His Excellency," someone bellowed.

"The governor," Bella shouted. "Oh, Mum, can't you see?"

"Governor?" asked the brave Rebecca, stopping on the path, kicking sideways at her skirts, though she knew, of course. "Governor of what?"

"Call the dog off," Bella shouted, "or we'll be in more trouble than we've got."

"The governor," growled Rebecca, "on my doorstep. Who'd believe that?"

"What's wrong with you, Mum? Call the dog off. It's the governor. Don't you understand that?"

"I understand perfectly, Bella. He thinks he's come to fill his coffers to pay his serfs. They all make me sick."

"They'll shoot White Dog," Bella cried, "if you don't call him off."

"They'd better not try," she said, and shrieked at White Dog across the gap.

"Enough. Enough. Enough. Enough."

White Dog went to earth in their midst, growling and bristling in their midst, while horses and men backed off.

"Good dog," murmured the brave Rebecca.

A powerful voice launched back. "His Excellency, madam, presents his respects."

"Well," she shouted, "if he presents them when Seth isn't here, if he comes like a thief, he provokes what he gets. Let him present his respects himself. I have nothing to say to serfs."

"Madam, I *do* present them myself."

The butt of her musket was still tucked into her hip. The muzzle didn't drop. "Put the kettle on, Bella," said Rebecca. "What about the shortbread? It's the governor, and he speaks for himself."

"Please, Mum," said Bella. "Please, Mum."

Again she shouted, "You may come to the house. Dismount carefully, and come quietly, or the dog may take fright."

She turned on her heel and made her way to her door, turned her back on the Queen's man.

It can't be true, thought Bella. She wouldn't dare treat him with contempt. But surely he wouldn't come for gold? Surely he couldn't believe that? Surely she'll behave herself?

In came the governor ahead of his aides, riding whip in hand tapping against his thigh, down that long path rutted by cart tracks, past the red currants, past the green beans and the potato crops, past the cow bale and the poultry run, past the tethered goats.

The proud woman stood at the door to her house of mud and slabs and bark. A ditch encircled the house, like a moat. Clematis climbed the walls and grass grew on the roof.

"Mrs. Gray," the governor said.

"Your Excellency."

"Madam, we have things to discuss."

"Take care then," she said, "as you cross the ramp."

She disappeared into the dark and he crossed after her and stooped to enter, an aide with him, an aide with a pistol. Rebecca observed the pistol and placed her musket on the table, close to her open hand.

"Please sit," she said, and he sat opposite her, the aide at his side, the aide's head close to the smoked beams of the roof.

The governor removed his gloves, slowly, slowly, and

breathed heavily, and looked into her eyes as they caught the light, and was gradually alerted to the room about, its simplicity, its bric-a-brac, its floor of hard-beaten earth. And aware of the girl near the hearth.

What a house, he thought. For a woman like this.

"Madam," he said, "your son Custard . . . am I to believe *you* gave a human being a name like that?"

"I called him Cuthbert, for his grandfather, who fell at Waterloo when you were a child underfoot."

The governor frowned. "Madam, I was at Waterloo, also, as you're well aware. Rudeness makes for a poor start."

"There are things," she said, "that I know nothing of. So you were at Waterloo. Back in 1826 I visited Chipping Sodbury with my aunt. Did you know that?"

The governor thought long about it, then said, "Your son Cuthbert is a political issue."

"My son Cuthbert is dead."

"Dead or alive, madam, who can say? Suffice for the moment, you should know I have feelings about it, or I wouldn't be here. But first tell me about the gold that started all this."

"What gold is that?"

"What gold is what?" he snapped. "You know well what I mean."

"I know what I think you mean, and I imagine you've come for your share, along with everyone else."

The aide coughed.

The governor went on, "If I were interested in your gold

in a material sense, I would legally take it, for everything above the earth and below it in Her Majesty's realm belongs to Her Majesty, and to remove it without her permission is theft."

"I might challenge her, sir, on that!"

"If it's gold that you've found, lady, through the agency of your remarkable child, and you've been irresponsible enough to chatter or boast, I've something else to worry about."

"I have uttered no word of the matter, sir, privately or publicly, except my opinion of absolute disbelief that grown-up men could attend to such nonsense."

He ignored her. "I am referring, madam, to the recent fact of the California gold rush."

Rebecca shrugged to that.

"You've heard of its lawlessness and violence and murder."

"I've heard of all these things," she said, "much closer to home than that, as you would know if you had prepared for this encounter, and without gold rushes to set them off."

"The gold, madam. I want a straight answer."

"You've had your straight answer."

He sighed.

"Let's clear a few things. I haven't called upon you without proper thought, or proper cause, or proper preparation, or proper *hesitation* I might add. Your fame, so to speak, having gone before you. Allow me to state what I know. Allow me to seek your confirmation. Five desperadoes, armed with knives and clubs, descended upon you here last

October and by force removed your son."

"*Six* desperadoes," said the brave Rebecca.

"*Five* desperadoes, madam; the youngest but fourteen years of age, the oldest eighteen. The following morning, most fortuitously, but as was his frequent habit, Thomas Button arrived on your doorstep."

"Thomas Button, sir, was a man of God, calling upon this household, as upon many other households, in the course of his work as pastor."

"As you have it, madam; as you have it. Nevertheless he came, released you and your daughter from your bonds, and expressing outrage at the indignities you had suffered and his fears for your son, vowed to follow those desperadoes and bring your son back again. Am I right, or am I misinformed?"

"That," said Rebecca, "is more or less as it was."

"And you have heard nothing of your son, or of Preacher Tom, from that day to this?"

"My son," said Rebecca, "is dead, and I fear that Preacher Tom is dead also."

"Accept my reassurance, madam, that at last report both were doing well."

"I don't know what you mean."

"There is a further complication, madam. Preacher Tom is the father of the desperadoes who took away your son."

"That is absurd."

"I am governor of this colony, God help me, and not given to absurdities. And there are other matters I would mention. Not only are all *those* persons missing—your son and Preacher Tom and his family—but a first-ranking collection of roughnecks and convict riffraff. More missing persons are listed at this date than I have seen in all my past years in this blighted place."

"Amen to that," said Rebecca, "and now he proceeds to assassinate the character of our dear friend and pastor and associate his name with criminals. Pour the tea, Bella."

"It's not time for tea," the governor barked.

"It is, if I say so, in my house."

"My God," said the governor.

It's the governor, thought Bella. It's himself. Our mother's mad. We've got the governor in our very own house, a real living *sir*, and she practically throws him out.

"I wish to be left to speak with this woman." The governor was looking at his aide and turning to Bella. "Out. Out."

He was breathing roughly and running a high colour and saying to himself, *what's a woman like this doing in a mud hut?*

"Bella," said Rebecca, "you are in your own house and are not being asked by me to leave it."

"I'd better go, Mum." She was burning up with embarrassment.

"If it's your wish."

I'd run a mile, thought Bella, if I could. He'll lock her up. He'll put her in jail.

Out burst Bella into the sunshine, swinging on her sticks, swinging away, past the soldiers and the horses.

"Missie," they called.

She went away from them, swinging away.

"In this colony, madam," said the governor to Rebecca, "I speak for Her Majesty. In your house I have the same voice and anticipate the same respect. You're not high enough in the realm, madam, for your rudeness to be considered quaint."

"I'm high here, sir, and make you no mistake."

He remained angry and nonplussed. "I repeat my question. I wait for the answer. You are required to answer. The gold?"

"And I repeat my reply. I know nothing of what you speak."

"The gold you've removed from the Queen's earth! You must have done so, or this fever of rumour in every tavern and on every street corner could not have come about. Do you imagine I live in an ivory tower?"

"It's a free country, sir," said Rebecca, "for those in high places, to hear as they wish and say as they wish and do as they wish. I'm told it's a privilege you guard jealously."

"You are as *free*, madam, as any person I've ever met! What you say is ridiculous. And what you add is insolent."

"And you, sir, will not order me to your will or call me a liar under my own roof, by the Queen's privilege or anyone else's privilege. Who is she, to insult me by proxy in my own house?"

"My God," said the governor, and closed his eyes for a period of escape. "I'm not here to harass you. I'm a man with a problem and you're a part of it, as are the others of whom I spoke. I'm concerned for the law and order of this land, for the security and safety of every one of us, for the right of masters to receive a day's work from the men they hire, and for the duty of workers to offer themselves for employment. The only place for gold in a community of this kind is in the ground, and the deeper the better. The gold of this world, madam, even of civilized lands, is stained with blood—the blood of the guilty and the blood of the innocent, the blood of the poor *and* the blood of the rich. Half the population of this colony have criminal origins, including your preacher friend! Are you hearing me?"

"I expect so," she said.

"This is why I beg of you, madam, to tell me if gold has been found. I don't seek to take it from you, though it would be safer in my vaults. I seek only to govern in a proper manner."

"I've told you already. I tell you again. They're all mad. There isn't any gold."

"When your son Seth is drunk, madam, that's not the story we hear."

"When my son is drunk," she said, "my son is drunk."

The governor sighed and Rebecca poured tea for him and offered the shortbreads and sat herself down as if unconcerned, though fearing that the hammering of her heart must be heard as far away as Sydney Town.

"Let's clear a point," the governor said. "You tell me Cuthbert is dead. I say there isn't a fool in the land who'd kill the Golden Goose, at least before it lays the golden egg."

"Golden Goose?" she said.

"It's what they call your Cuthbert, madam. The rum shops ring with the fame of his name. I'm surprised your drunken son has not brought talk of it home."

"You'll not call my Seth drunken."

"I've yet to hear of him sober, madam."

He watched her carefully, but she bore the wound with dignity. "If gold were to be found in this country," she said, "someone would have found it long ago."

"In that event, madam, someone would have hushed it up long ago. Take my word for it. We'd have had thousands of convicts running crazy. Murder and mayhem, madam. Not a free man or woman left to do an honest day's work for an honest day's pay. The whole structure of society cut away. Think of it. Sentencing criminals for life to an El Dorado. A perverse and dangerous justice that would be."

There sat the brave Rebecca.

"I have a theory about Preacher Tom. His sons carried Cuthbert off, for they were not known to you, and he came next morning to fox you, to disarm you, to cover the tracks. A clumsy plan, ineptly conceived and untidily executed, with evidence of incrimination left lying all over the place, but he's a simple man."

There were tears in her eyes.

"What has happened since, madam, God knows, though if your son is not alive I know nothing of human nature.

Your son is gold in the bank. Whoever has him is feeling pretty good about life."

"It's ridiculous."

"I don't think so."

"It's ridiculous!"

She began to weep.

"I want your son back, Mrs. Gray, in your care, safe, sound, and secure from mischief. If there's to be a gold rush in this colony, it'll be on my terms, not on terms of chaos or anarchy. I'm about to offer a reward for your son. Two hundred pounds is the sum I have in mind, and it's my duty to acquaint you with my intention, and to invite you to add to it yourself."

There she sat.

There sat the brave Rebecca.

There she sat, expressionless.

He had a reputation with the ladies. He was notorious.

"You may be sure, madam, I *would* have sent my serfs, had I not wished to confront for myself the lady who shot Kinsella Smith, and whose spirit is as much discussed as her marksmanship."

There sat the brave Rebecca, already miles off. "In your estimation, in what direction lies my son?" she said.

Her anger was like a tempest.

chapter three

THE PROCLAMATION

Victoria Regina
£200 REWARD
for Information leading
to the Capture of
The Button Gang:
Thomas Button, 61 years, known as Preacher Tom,
And the Sons of Thomas Button known as
Jamie the Captain, 18 years
Kenrick van der Mellow Mere, 17 years
Hector the Lady Killer, 16 years
and Little Lou, 14 years
Also Frederick Hopper, 18 years
(known as Cousin Fred or Whistling Fred)
FURTHERMORE, AN ADDITIONAL £200
REWARD FOR
the Safe Return of Cuthbert, 13 years
known as Custard
son of Mrs. Rebecca Gray
Kidnapped by the Button Gang from Inglewood
in the Colony of New South Wales

By His Excellency's Command, 1st February, 1851

chapter four

MISTRESS OF THE HOUSE

At last they heard Seth coming from market. At last they heard the rattle of the cart as it came bumping through the forest across tree roots standing up like cross rails, exposed by wear and weather at the edges of the track, or as wheels dropped into pits made by spring rains, though spring had long gone and much of summer as well.

Seth was singing his song.

On the way to market, yesterday, laden with the things he had grown, Seth avoided the roots and the holes, because then he saw them and cared about it. Nothing mattered now, not even getting home. Black Dog took the care. Black Dog would get him there, safe and sound, and the cart horse knew the way.

So Seth sang his song, the song his father used to sing, though the words were not the same.

"He's drunk," Rebecca said.

But that was nothing new.

"He's drunk," she said, as if it had not happened before, though rarely had she spoken it aloud and never had she required him to give account. She'd help him down, her gorgeous Seth, her gorgeous son, so like his father before him, and feed him black tea and oatmeal biscuits and put him to bed. That's what she would have done at any other time.

"He's drunk," she said.

It was a mood in her mother that Bella hadn't seen until this last half-day, until the hours had begun to come and begun to go, and evening had taken the place of day, and stars had appeared like hard bright points of anger.

No one had eaten and the cooking fire was black and the lantern was not alight at the door.

"For once," Rebecca said, "couldn't he have brought home a straight thought in a straight head?"

She strode to the well and drew from its depths two buckets of dark water almost as cold as a winter frost.

Seth was coming, singing his song.

> To market, to market, I took the fat hen,
> O-jolly-o, jolly-o.
> Silver for feathers and gold for her egg,
> Hey diddle duddle, the kit and the fuddle-o.
> Rum for her master,
> Booze by the barrel-o.
> Loverly, loverly, loverly jolly-o,
> How-do-you-do and a very amen.

"Get down," said Rebecca.

"Is that my mother?" said Seth, from somewhere among the clouds where he soared with the eagles. "Is that the incredible Rebecca of whom everyone speaks?"

"Get down," said Rebecca, and reached up to the body of his shirt and wrenched.

Seth toppled over the footboard, over the shafts, onto

his shoulders, and spread like a half-filled bag of earth, as if his body lacked bones, and Black Dog made sounds that brought from Rebecca a snarl, "Be off with you, Black Dog."

"No, Mum; no, Mum," Bella murmured, but to herself, wanting to turn her back, wanting to be somewhere else.

"Take care of the horse, Bella. I want him fed and watered and groomed. Let me see you do it."

Seth was crawling into the dark and his mother went after him, a bucket in each hand, slopping and splashing, and she flushed the lot into his face.

"Gawd love us," he shrieked, "she's gone mad." For he had expected her to steady him to the ground and to take his arm and help him into the house, an indulgence of some satisfaction to them both.

My son, Rebecca wept inside herself. My gorgeous Seth. You might be a strong and beautiful man, but I despise you tonight, that you would do this to yourself, to your beautiful body and your beautiful brain, that you would care so little for yourself, that you would betray your mother and your brother. That you would betray the one who cannot care for himself. That you would lie and boast, and bring your mother who adores you to this moment of truth and of hate.

"Get up," she said.

His retching sounds disgusted her.

"Get up!"

"Mum," cried Bella, from somewhere out in the dark. "Have pity on him. He can't."

"Get up!"

She threw an empty bucket that struck him on the hip, and he crawled farther into the dark, and she went back to the well, and drew more water, and attacked him again.

"I despise you," she said.

He clawed to his feet as if clawing up a hill. He was drenched and astonished and frightened.

He had to plant his feet apart, wide apart, had to flex and fight against every drugged muscle and sinew to stay upright, for he knew that his mother was a violent woman, but never in his twenty years and eighty days had she directed that violence against him, until here, until now.

It was an awful noise in his head.

"Scum," she said.

He tried to grope with the shock of that; tried to grope towards a comprehension of it.

"Your brother was taken from here," she said, "because of things you said and things you did. You've betrayed us. You've betrayed him. You're a fool. And why have you not told me that they speak of him in the alehouses as if he survives? As he does. Yesterday, in my house, the governor of the colony. Yesterday the Queen's man told me so himself. He told me that you had betrayed your brother. He told me you were a drunken lout. He told me that Preacher Tom had betrayed us all. Our Preacher Tom. The Button Gang. Our own Preacher Tom."

She swung the flat of her hand at Seth and struck him on the cheek. Like a gunshot was the sound, the sound of the slap and the sound of his gasp.

He fell.

"I say to you, Seth Gray, that you stay on this side of that gate and care for your sister Bella, as she will care for you, until I bring your brother back. It's a man's job, but who could entrust a man's job to a drunken lout? You will leave this property under no circumstance. You will allow the crops to rot in the ground. If you disobey me, I'll disown you and drive you out.

"Get to your feet."

He struggled up and she struck him a second time with the same force.

An hour later she rode out into the dark, rode the cart horse, rode him bareback, rode him packed for a long journey, White Dog going with her.

"I fulfil my vow," she said.

Bella listened at the gate until the last faint sound had become part of the body of the night.

She swung back up the track, swinging on her sticks, mistress of the house.

chapter five

SONS OF THE POOR

HOW MANY RIVERS had they crossed? How many mountains had they climbed? How many campfires had they made?

How long ago was it that Prospector Tom and Custard had left the sea behind, the sea for sitting in and leaping in and running wild? If you were the size of a kid, that is, not the size of a man, six feet four or even more, with a tall black hat on top of it all and a Bible in a box as big as a paving stone.

Sixty days? Ninety days? Or years and years and years?

How far behind were the cliffs along the shore, the cliffs for rolling down and falling from and scampering up on all fours? And the bandit kingdom of Ruratoria hidden below like a pearl, where Custard had been sixth-in-command and the four sons of Prospector Tom and Whistling Fred had been living in style. Living on cheese and ham. Not getting up in the morning until you reckoned it was time.

Strangers might have walked the sands and never guessed that the desperadoes were hidden there, chewing on their lumps of cheese, dreaming their marvellous dreams, and had claimed the world as their very own for as far as they

could see, that being the right of the young and hearty and
clear of eye, and Queen Victoria hadn't sent the soldiers
to wrest it back again. Perhaps she hadn't heard, and what
she hadn't heard about didn't trouble her at night when
she was counting up the countries that she owned.

"Sixteen countries jumping over the fence. Seventeen
countries jumping over the fence. Eighteen countries jumping over the fence. . . . What's this, what's this, what's
this here? Some renegade kingdom in the middle of my
very own?"

"I command the frying pan," Custard had declared, so long
ago, so far away, to the sons of Prospector Tom gathered
there, in their very own secret lair. Well, as much as one
can keep a secret of that kind. As much as one can keep a
secret of *any* kind.

"We've captured him," they said, before they became
scared, before the world started falling down. "We've captured the kid who can find the gold by waving his pieces
of wood. Well, that's what our dad says when he comes
home from his preaching and his riding around, and is
telling us stories of the travels he's made and the people
he's seen and the things he's done.

"Now we'll be rich as kings," they said, "because the
kid can wave his magic sticks and we'll buy all sorts of
wonderful things. A house to live in and a ship to sail in
and horses and carriages and coats with red silk linings and
a piano for Whistling Fred.

"Well, it's our very own dad," they said, "that's what he says. They drive the spade down and up it comes, gold shining in the dirt, gold shining in the mud, and this kid's mum, she drops it in the box that's barred all round with bronze and bolts and hides it under her bed."

"The frying pan," said Custard, after they'd brought him to the cave and showed him where he'd live, "that's what I'll command if you want me to join the gang."

But he hadn't eaten his first piece of ham before everything was finished, before everything was done.

Down came the great voice, the great force descending, greater than freedom, greater than having a gang of your own, greater than heads full of exciting ideas of what you'd do when you were a rich and famous man.

"He's coming," the bandit captain wailed.

"Who's coming?" rose the cry.

"The devil man to burn us alive."

Down through the hills on his small grey horse the devil man came, his tall black hat bobbing around. Over the cliff he came, ranting and roaring, sand and stones pattering down.

"Scum," roared the devil man, as the bandits fled from a father's rage.

Poor desperadoes, dreams all dismayed.

> Devil man, devil man,
> Why did you come?
> We were the bandit gang
> Jumping for fun.

"Curd of man," roared the devil man. "Dishonour on my name."

Oh, the ranting and the roaring. How terrible it was.

Custard and the bandit captain were left behind. Or something of the kind. Who can be sure of anything when bandit captains quail and everyone else has fled to the compass points, running and stumbling?

The devil man picked up the bandit captain and threw him against the wall of the lair. Oh crack. Oh crunch. Oh thud against the wall.

> Jamie Button,
> Jamie Button,
> Was that your woolly head?
> Jamie Button,
> Jamie Button,
> I fear you're deady dead.

"Fool," boomed the devil man, "what did you want to kidnap him for? They'll string you up by the neck until you are dead. Haven't you a brain or a wit in your head? And what have you done to me besides? Ruined my life and ruined my name. How could I raise such a clutch of fools?"

Or something like that was said.

So Preacher Tom snatched Custard up and rode away from the sea, rode away and rode away, beating at his brow and pleading with God. "I'm ruined, I'm ruined. How do I save my sons from the wrath of Rebecca, and the vengeance of the Law that wreaks such vengeance upon the sons of the poor? This dreadful thing they've done.

I cannot think. I cannot think. And I have vowed to Rebecca to find her son and take him to her back again. I cannot think. I cannot think."

Away he rode and away he rode.

"Father God, I pray thee, what must I do to save their necks? Oh my sons, and foolish, foolish Fred, growing up to commit such an infamous thing. I cannot think."

On he rode into the sun, day after day after day, into the great mountains, on and on.

"They'll call me Prospector Tom," he said to Custard. "It is better that they should. Preacher once, perhaps Preacher again, but not for a time. And we'll journey on, you and I, you the servant at my command and I the servant of the Lord, and perhaps they'll call me the Benefactor, the Discoverer of Gold. Shall God in His mercy do this for me, for I have served Him and suffered for Him these many long years?

"Open up the coffers of the Earth, Father God, I entreat Thee. There is no other way for the likes of us.

"Then I'll buy *freedom* for my sons.

"I'll go to the Law-makers and say, 'It is well known there is one law for the rich and another for the poor, by which the poor are sentenced, by which the poor are hung, and by which the rich go free. I am the Discoverer of Gold. Give my sons to me.'

"And gold there'll be for the poor, for the hungry, for the down-trodden. My heart breaks for the wretches of this land. Gold there will be for them, such gold as was never seen by the rich.

"And the people will rise and shout, *Honour to Pros-pector Tom, the Blessed One, who changed our desperate land to the grandest place you ever saw. Honour to his family name. Honour instead of shame.*"

Stumbling behind was Custard, hair like rough-cut straw blowing wild in the wind, legs aching fit to fall off, mumbling and grumbling and thinking up songs in which Prospector Tom dropped dead.

> Dead as I don't know,
> Dead as Romeo,
> Deader deader yet,
> Dead as Juliet.
>
> Deader deader die,
> Dead as putrefy,
> Dead as shockin' smell,
> Dead as rot in Hell.

And he sang other songs of the same kind, but under his breath. There was no point in being the dead one himself.

First passed the plains beyond the sea, then the mountains on and on.

Where was home? Where had it gone? Who could find it, ever again?

Then plains for another time, or ravines with falling rocks, or raging rivers, or wastelands like the mazes of a dream. Such a vastness it was. Like a continuing *amen*.

"Stop right here," Prospector Tom would cry.

Little Horse would make a sighing sound, as if thanking the Horse God, because he'd have spent half the day climbing some cliff, or struggling through some rugged pass, or choking in a dust cloud, carrying half the weight of the world on his back.

"Sighhhhh," said Little Horse.

"Grumble rumble mumble," said Custard, or that was what it sounded like, then drew his knife and cut another stick.

chapter six

ABOUT STICKS

A NICE LITTLE STICK, thin and supple, with a fork in it, each fork as long as his hand measured twice, and the stem as long as his arm measured once. Not that it mattered, though everyone thought it did.

If he held a straight stick out in front, it worked just as well; it'd tremble, it'd quiver, it'd bend even double; but why tell them? Custard liked to keep a little bit of mystery for himself.

"A nice forked stick looks well," Mum used to say, back in the long-ago days when he was still discovering his tricks with sticks. "It's an ancient art, son, finding these invisible streams of water, and forked sticks, they tell us, down through the ages, have done the job best. So do it right, son. When God gives you such a wonderful gift, it's up to you to present it with elegance."

Nice word that. Custard liked it.

I'm elegant, he'd think, and when no one else was around he'd look haughty and mince his steps and sweep about the place majestically and say to the trees, "I'm King Custard, King of the Sticks, and you're just a piece of wood."

"Making the best of what you've got," Mum used to go

on, "is an act of worship, so to speak. You don't have to get down on your knees and make a holy fuss. You don't have to stand on the rooftops and wave your arms and shout. God can hear you, God can see you, without your help. He knew all about you before you took your first step."

"*All* about me? You mean like *everything?*"

"Of course, and why not? You've nothing to hide or nothing to fear."

She doesn't know the half of it, thought Custard.

"So," said Mum, "when each of us finds out what it is, this special gift that God has given us—because to each of us He's given something—we *use* it to its very best. There's no better way of saying *thank you* to God."

Which was probably why, Custard reckoned, she was such a good shot when she was shooting at men, because she had so much practice at it, because God expected her not to miss. So he'd take out his knife with the lovely shiny blade, the one Mum had given him for the very purpose, and he'd hold it close to his mouth and spit on it.

Glop.

Then back and forth he'd hone it, across the seat of his pants, swush-swush swush-swush, taking care not to get the blade on edge, because that could have been real dangerous.

Or, if there'd been too much spit, and that depended upon the weather, there'd be a noise that sounded more like *schlop*.

"That'll do," Prospector Tom usually said, sounding

quite abrupt. "Get on with it, will you! That knife's sharp enough to sever an elephant's neck."

Sharp enough to go straight through yours, anyway, Custard used to think, and I'll bet you wouldn't bleed a drop. Words would come out, out they'd pour, knee deep.

"If you want me to do it right, like me mum says, I've got to find the right stick. Then I've got to cut it right. Then it's got to be in tune with the place. If it's the wrong stick it won't work. Everything's got to be right."

"Your mother calls you simple," Prospector Tom had been known to growl, sounding a bit like a bear in the bush. "You've got her hoodwinked. It's all an act. Simple, my fat aunt. You're a fiend. You're a child of the devil, I reckon. I say you're Little Nick."

Well, if the devil's me dad, thought Custard, I've got a real famous father, haven't I?

Swush-swush, he'd go with the knife, on the seat of his pants, hissing through his teeth, then he'd hold the knife up to the light and squint along the edge of it and maybe have another spit, aiming for the ground, though not necessarily hitting it, because his aim over distances wasn't all that good. Prospector Tom used to stand clear, having learnt from experience early on.

So Custard would peel off the bark at the tip, in a patient way, and start bending the stick in different directions and the man would get madder and madder.

"You'll break it."

"I won't."

"If you *do* break it, I'll clout you."

"There's plenty more. The bush is full of them. Look at them. All over the place. Hangin' on every tree in sight."

"Get on with it, kid."

Used to sound real coarse, he did, just the way Seth used to. Seth used to jump up and down on the spot, tearing at his hair, screaming and shouting, "Get on with it. Stir yourself. Wake up. Jump to it. Get a wriggle on. Can't you move an inch?"

Well, yeh, a fellow could from time to time, if it became a matter of life or death.

"If you go turning up more water this time," Prospector Tom would get round to saying, "I'll up-end you in it and *drown* you in it. And if you find any more bones I'll beat you brainless with 'em. Never known a country like it, I haven't. Never seen so many bones. More dead people livin' here than livin' in the rest of the world, I reckon."

"Never had nothing else to do with their time," said Custard, "except die. They had to do something, didn't they?"

"Get on with it. Get on with it! *Get on with it!*"

So off Custard would go, wandering in circles or off on straight lines or in little squares or zigzags, as the fancy moved him, with a fork of the stick held by a thumb in each palm, and all sorts of strange looks on his face, following Mum's advice, to make the best of it. He'd wrinkle his nose and twitch the corners of his mouth and puff at the flies and wriggle his ears and Prospector Tom would be saying, as was his habit, "Haven't you felt it yet?"

"No."

"Can't understand it. Looks like the perfect spot to me. Felt myself guided here by the spirit, I did. Can't you feel *anything?*"

"No."

"Strange. Strange."

When he really felt it, which wasn't often, it was a bit like getting scorched or something, or having a fright and not knowing what you were frightened of.

"Can't you feel anything yet?"

"No."

Or standing too close to a wheel that was going round, or getting bitten by a bee, or knocking your funny bone.

"Feeling anything yet?"

"No."

If the water was running he'd know. If it was lying in a pool he'd know. It was a different feeling for different things. If it was a human skull he'd get the galloping gallumpings.

"You're *still* not feeling anything?"

"Yeh, yeh!" And all of a sudden down would go the end of the stick, all of a quiver, and he'd yell, "Dig here, dig here," and off he'd trot to the nearest log as fast as he could scuttle, making sure there weren't any snakes or bull-ants about, and he'd settle with a satisfied sigh.

Back in the early days Prospector Tom used to do the digging, until he started thinking more seriously about the defects of the situation. Down he'd dig through rock and clay, through the most incredible stuff, swinging his pick, throwing his shovel about, sweating and grunting and wincing and panting for breath, getting blisters and a sore back and skinned knees and bruised elbows and cricks in his shoulders and the stomachache, because having been a preacher for so long he'd got out of the way of digging holes.

Down he'd dig and down he'd dig, sometimes disappearing from sight, while Custard sat on his log, scratching himself, swatting at passing insects, day-dreaming, or making up songs that he didn't risk singing aloud.

Out round the edges of the farmlands, during the early days, far from curious eyes, Prospector Tom dug his holes. "Today," he'd say, "today, today. Today's the day we strike it rich."

But it wasn't.

Then up through the foothills and on into the mountains, mile after mile, week after week, away from all the roads where travellers passed, hole after hole, leaving behind a brand-new batch of fresh-water springs and heaps of bones and even the odd bit of iron, but never a speck of gold, while Custard dozed on his log or made up his songs or wiggled his toes.

Prospector Tom even struck springs that Custard hadn't known were there, because it was easy enough to fake the twitch of the stick, especially when he was tired and wanted to sit down. But times changed and Custard stopped giving false alarms after he had dug a couple of holes himself. Hoeing the row back home on the farm was easy compared with hacking holes in the sides of mountains, was even easier than hacking out holes on the plain. Must have been made of iron, that plain, a dreadful place it was, getting harder and hotter all the time. Prospector Tom started breaking pick handles trying to make dints in it.

The water didn't flow any more. The creek beds were dry and dust blew. Water was deep deep down, away out of sight, quiet and dark, hiding in the cool earth, and finding it was more a matter of luck, or of remaining alert for places where black men had camped.

Black men knew where the waters were. They'd had thousands of years to find out. But they had no use for gold.

chapter seven

WORDS WRITTEN
DIFFERENT WAYS

PROSPECTOR TOM'S BIBLE was a book in a box as big as a paving stone.

The black man's Bible was the land; the whole land; the breadth and depth and height of it; the heart and soul of it; the whole land.

The chapter and verse of Prospector Tom's Bible lived in his passions and in his mind, for his sight was not what it had been and even before the sun went down the words were blurred, as if a mesh came between his eyes and the page.

Everything was different at night. Different from day. Oh, different, different.

As day began to go, as night began to come, the land changed, the plain changed, everything changed.

All around presences came, forms arose, feelings turned into masses that were invisible by day but filled the night with towers and mountains.

Custard's heart beat faster then. Perhaps it always had, even on the farm, when the sun went down. Even the farm was part of the same strange land. Even the bones he found. They were the bones of black men and black women and black children; the bones of the guardians of the land. He disturbed the bones and mists came up and followed him.

At night when Prospector Tom kindled the evening fire and prepared the dough, the mists gathered closer, just outside the glow.

They sat around.

Custard couldn't quite see them. They were just outside his range. They were like breezes; real things that you couldn't see. All you could feel was the chill. All you noticed was the movement of the leaves.

After a time Prospector Tom would unlatch the box and remove the Bible and open it upon a grey blanket at his side and spread his right hand across the page. Under his fingertips in the dark were a million words.

The power, the magic, and the majesty of the words.

The chapter and verse of the black man's Bible lived in the boulders and the watercourses and the bluffs and the knolls and the plains, and could not be moved. Everywhere the black man turned he saw his sacred shapes and his sacred stones.

The power and the magic and the majesty of the land were desecrated because Prospector Tom was there and dug holes.

Custard knew that at night Prospector Tom read his Bible through his memory and his hands. And he knew why, for at night the whole land moved, and was hostile;

the very stones and the very bones stirred. Custard felt the touch of feet on the land, as if the land were part of his own flesh, feet that crept, feet that paused. He felt their rising up and their closing in, felt the eyes all around.

On the horizon, fires glowed.

Custard tried not to see them. Trying not to see fires didn't send them away.

He'd listen. He'd strain. There would be all kinds of tightenings inside him. There were sounds. There were songs with simple rhythms. Hands were clapping. Rhythms were beating. But not a word could he understand because of the miles.

He'd sit up with a start. "Tell me a story."

Prospector Tom would tell of Samuel perhaps, Samuel the boy, listening in the dark thousands of years ago to the voice of the Lord, as Custard himself would listen, anxiously, as the story paused.

Or Prospector Tom would tell of David the shepherd boy, hiding from the madness of King Saul. How had he got to be a king if he was mad? And of Jonathan, son of King Saul, David's friend.

That was nice; the bit about David's friend.

So Custard would get to thinking of Hector, his own friend, Hector the bandit, who was nice to him on the cliff beside the sea, the only friend of his entire, complete, personal own, for no one young lived near the farm at home. Except maybe Bella, and she was his sister, and bossed him around.

Hector, the son of Tom Button the Preacher, the Pros-

pector, the man whose face he saw in the glow of the coals.
The very same nose, the noble Roman nose.

Or perhaps he'd hear of Noah the builder, who built not
only the boat, but started the world again after the old
world drowned in the flood.

Or of Samson the strong, with muscles like the boles of
trees, who pulled the house down on his very own head.
What a fall. All those beams and all those pillars and all
those ceilings crashing down.

Or he'd hear the voice of Prospector Tom turn loud and
hollow, like a voice in a cellar. And he'd fall asleep again,
leaving Prospector Tom on his own, leaving him alone,
out in the cold of the strange land.

The spirits listened then, and the moths about the coals
listened until they fell in and were consumed, and the
eternal rustling silence of the land listened, and the horizon
glow listened, and Prospector Tom's uneasiness grew like
something growing rampant with thorns, for he knew that
his stories left the land unmoved.

"I wish I was home," his spirit said, "in the soft light
and the soft grass and the soft rain. It's been such a long
time, all the long years in this land."

Then something would scream.

Oh, a shattering *alien* scream, as if something had been
caught up by the throat and beaten brainless into the
ground. The scream dying. The scream becoming part of
the silence as the boy stirred, having heard it in his dream,
his mouth drawing great drafts of healing air.

The silence of this awful, ancient land, wherein no

cities had ever stood, wherein no fields of ripening corn had ever grown, wherein no person had written a single word.

Alien was the land. And alien was he, was the man.

Oh, the hours of turning and bruising and waiting for the distant, distant dawn.

Oh, of *nothing* that he could do with himself; of a lifetime between each sunset and dawn, while the boy slept, while the fire beside them was the only visible wall against the malice of this awful land.

Oh, the blessing of the dawn . . .

In the light of day Prospector Tom strode on and out to find the golden El Dorado.

"I am the man who will find it. God has chosen me. Why should this land sleep and not yield its fruit? God said the earth was for man to subdue."

But his feet came to earth like a cat's and his ears were pricked like a cat's and he was as alert as a cat in every nerve.

God was his shield. A fool might ask for God's protection, but ignore the rules of survival and lose his blood on the ground.

Along came Custard, stumbling behind.

A pact between God and man worked two ways, as Prospector Tom himself had preached in former days, thundering from the tree stumps, the crowds gathering round, for he was a wonderful showman in a land short on shows and they came in from far and wide to watch him perform.

"Let me tell you about God's doctrine of the fair swap.

Give what you ask for and get it back. Good for good, or evil for evil, that's what you'll get. A fair swap, God said at the beginning, when he laid down the rules, is always going to be a fair swap. So blame yourselves for your rotten stinkin' luck. Don't blame me, God said, if you don't spit on your hands and get it started for yourself. If you want bread for each day, He said, try planting wheat in the ground. If you'd be safe in the storm, He said, try building yourself a house with roof and walls, don't stand like a donkey out in the rain."

The night-time glow of fires followed him through the mountains and onto the plain.

There were times he could have sworn they were following him by design.

There were times when fires burnt almost all around.

There was the time when the great fire began and the sky in the day was red and the sky in the night was aflame.

"I am not secure," he confided to God.

But God was silent in those days.

chapter eight

SING GOLDEN GOOSE

MEN GATHERING in campfire circles were singing a new song that year, sometimes with a mouth organ or a whistle for the tune.

They were men on the march, burnt by wind and sun, lean from hardship.

> Old Tommy was the Preacher Man,
> Old Tommy was the parson,
> Preaching here and prancing there
> And promising damnation.

> Sing Golden Goose,
> Sing Golden Goose,
> Sing Golden Goose, my hearty.

And more were the verses and more were the choruses they sang and many were the campfires behind great boulders and great trees and in creek beds and round on the far sides of hills, haunting the night with fireglow on clouds.

> High he preached and low, my lads,
> All round the town and county,
> In and out the parlour doors
> Charming every lady.

Sing Golden Goose,
Sing Golden Goose,
Sing Golden Goose, my hearty.

They clapped their hands and slapped their thighs,
though some had muskets on their knees.

Lock up your daughters and your wives,
We serve all men the notice,
Or he'll sweep them off their feet
And God'll reign triumphant.

Sing Golden Goose,
Sing Golden Goose,
Sing Golden Goose, my hearty.

Now he's off to make it, lads,
To find the El Dorado,
Back he'll come as rich as sin,
A feather in his hat, sir.

Sing Golden Goose,
Sing Golden Goose,
Sing Golden Goose, my hearty.

Lock up your wives and daughters, lads,
The Preacher Man will get them,
Rich he'll be and richer he
Than Albert and the Queen, sir.

Sing Golden Goose,
Sing Golden Goose,
Sing Golden Goose, my hearty.

chapter nine

TIME FOR MIRACLES

STANDING HIGH upon a rock one day, round about noon, that splendid preacher fellow started prophesying to the blistering winds of Hell.

Oh, a shocking day it was, but a most splendid rock with a nice flat top for standing on.

Here we go again, thought Custard, when I should be having me lunch.

"The Bible tells us," said Prospector Tom, looking king-like up there on his rock, looking down at Custard and clearing at his throat, "that there's a time for all things; a time for suffering and a time for miracles, and a time for shouting out loud, and all mornin' I've felt the urge coming on. A most rewarding feeling reserved for those in communion with the Lord, what others know nothing about, that God has remembered again, that your prayers have got through, that the road's wide open. 'Well done, faithful servant,' He's been saying. 'You've stuck to it through thick and thin. You've proved yourself upon the sword of adversity. You've won the prize of the gorgeous golden reef.' "

Goodness, thought Custard, standing up straighter, stretching his neck like a swan. *Really* stretching it. What's that I see?

"So," the great voice rang, "it's the land of promise we've come to, where the gold lies waiting, given to us by our Father God in one of His gracious moments, and until this hour no fella like me ever having clapped eyes upon it, or set foot upon it, or come so close to bein' the richest fella you ever did see."

Well I never, thought Custard, just look at that! With me very own eyes I see *smoke!*

I mean *smoke,* as made by a fire what someone's lit.

A fire what someone sits beside, to toast his toes or toast his bread or boil his billy-can on.

By which time Prospector Tom had tucked his tall black hat into the crook of his arm and raised his right hand higher to bring God's attention closer. "Here blooms the flower, my boy, of your mysterious power, my boy, so cut a bright new stick and get busy."

Do you reckon *smoke* could mean a *trooper,* thought Custard, come to save me, come to hit Ole Tommy on the head?

"O my Father God," called Prospector Tom up there on his rock, "as Moses climbed the Mount to speak with Thee in the desert, far from the taverns and the bawdy houses, hear the plea of Thy servant Thomas and through me establish the Age of Justice. Let Thy gifts come through me to the poor and destitute and innocent in prison, and all shall praise Thee with me, because I'll be lining them up on Sundays and making sure of it, I promise. You getting busy with that stick down there, kid? I don't see much movement."

Smoke in broad daylight, thought Custard, close enough to get to!

"Hey," yelled Prospector Tom, "can't you hear me down there?"

Someone's sending me a signal, thought Custard, from down there in those trees. Over here, they're saying, come on over this way, kid, and we'll save you from that terrible ole fella.

Well, thought Custard, it's time I reckon. All this time waiting. Never seeing nothing but spooks and creepy-crawlies and black fellows hiding in the bushes.

I wonder what day it is, thought Custard, I wonder what month? I wonder whether I've had my birthday yet? Fancy not knowing how old I am. People'll think I'm stupid.

"Hey," bellowed Prospector Tom. "You down there, Little Nick, I'm talking to you."

"What you talking to me for?" said Custard.

"Julius Caesar," bellowed Prospector Tom. "Cut your-self a stick, will you, and get on with it!"

Impatient fella he is, thought Custard. So he spat on his knife and hissed a bit and honed the blade on the seat of his trousers and looked along the edge of it for a while and found a little wattle bush, no higher than himself, and cut a tidy little fork of green wood from it.

I've been through this so many times before, thought Custard. But he hasn't seen the smoke, has he? Bad luck for him. I'm not his watchdog, am I? I don't have to tell him, do I?

"Today's the day," yelled Prospector Tom, "and this is the hour. *So get on with it!*"

That smoke's no more than a mile away, I reckon, thought Custard. Can I get there before he does? His legs are so long, that Ole Tommy. Well, here goes anyway. I wish me knees would stop wobbling.

He stretched the forked stick across the palms of his hands and trotted away from the high-up ground down towards the hollow.

"Hey," yelled Prospector Tom. "Where are you off to?"

Custard went hurrying on, as if moving along a line that allowed for no diversion.

"Hey, wait," bellowed Prospector Tom. "What are you up to, little devil?"

Custard shouted, "It's pulling."

"It's *what?*"

"Pulling. Pulling."

"Holy Saint Cecilia," bellowed Prospector Tom. "Would you believe it? Hey, you wait on there a minute. You wait for your Uncle Thomas."

"Pulling like a bullock," shouted Custard.

"I'm coming. I'm coming."

"Yow," shouted Custard, "I can't hold it."

"It's happened," bellowed Prospector Tom. "It's gorgeous gorgeous happened. You wait there, little devil. It's me prayin' what's done it."

Off on a beeline went Custard, the smoke fixed in his mind like a marker, though the place itself had passed out of his vision, though his mouth was getting drier and drier and his breath was burning in his throat and his legs were hardly strong enough to stand on.

"Glory hallelujah," bellowed Prospector Tom. "Praise His name, the Merciful, the Giver of all things great and all things good and all things beautiful."

Down he scrambled from his rock, jamming on his hat, whistling up his horse, and heading out after Custard with strides five feet long at the shortest.

"I knew it, I knew it," he bellowed. "The day for signs and wonders. The day for miracles to happen. Gold by the bucket. Gold by the lump as big as barrels. You wait on there, little devil, little cherub, little angel. You wait on there, sweet Custard."

Running away was Custard, running away from him, running as fast as he could scamper.

"Never seen the like of it," bellowed Prospector Tom, his horse on the rein lurching after him, packs and pots and pans and shovels clattering.

"Remarkable," bellowed Prospector Tom. "Pulling like a bullock. Pulling us on to gorgeous, gorgeous fortune. Hang on it, young fellow, like life depended. Lift your pesky feet there, Little Horse, or I'll leave you to the crows. Shift your pesky carcase. Clippedy clop. Show 'em you can travel. Our precious boy is leading us on to the golden dawn of freedom."

Away went Custard, panic all around him rushing with him.

Here I come, Mr. Trooper.

Take me home, Mr. Trooper.

All I've got to do is last the distance.

As hard as he could run, ran Custard, flaming with heat and burning up for breath and hurting all over.

"Come back, little devil," bellowed Prospector Tom, a different kind of bellow, "or I'll beat the daylights out of you."

"Mr. Trooper," cried Custard, but the trees in the hollow were nowhere visible. The smoke must have been farther yet, as far as the fireglow of the evenings.

How could people vanish? How could they not hear him?

He ran across the slope and up the slope and down the slope. He crashed through scrub and swung round trees and thought he saw people through the torrents of his perspirings, through the spinnings of his senses, thought he saw bits of people, hands, feet, sometimes a shoulder.

Nothing came to him. Nothing was there when he reached it.

"I'm Custard, the kid who was kidnapped.

"You lit a fire. Can't you hear me?"

I saw the fire, thought Custard; I saw the smoke. I know I didn't imagine it.

"Save me," he cried, with the last of his strength, and went down on his knees and nursed his sick head and shook and rolled over and doubled up with groaning.

A mile was so far. Who'd ever have thought a mile was so far?

Now he'll hit me. Now he'll beat me. He'll pick me up like he picked up Jamie and throw me. Poor Custard. Poor Jamie.

A hand as big as an elephant, oh bigger, bigger, took him by the neck and wrenched him into the presence of the moment.

Groaning was Prospector Tom.

"Devil," he panted, and went on groaning, went on rasping, pressing at his sides and pressing at his heart, went on holding Custard like a chicken about to be strangled. "Don't ever try that again. Don't ever, ever try that again."

A hand like the recoil of a cannon came out of the glare and knocked Custard reeling amongst the boulders the earth was made of. Oh, they were harder than living. They were almost harder than dying.

He's thrown me like he threw Jamie.

Custard reeled, floundering, falling, shocked and crying.

"Devil," panted Prospector Tom with awesome passion. "You wouldn't have lasted a day. Don't you know you'd never have lasted a day? Don't you know you'd have perished?"

Custard lay crying.

It was a long time since he had cried about anything.

"Never, never run away again," groaned Prospector Tom. "Thirst'll kill you. Hunger'll kill you. Blacks'll kill you. How could you be so stupid?"

The man was groaning and gulping at the searing air and fearing for himself, for the awful effort he had called out of himself, but afraid even more that he could have lost the boy.

The storms inside of him.

The boy never heard a word. You talked, and talked, and he was far away, an age away, and never listened.

"Why did you do it?"

Custard only cried.

So it was that Prospector Tom smelt the crust of white man's flour baking in the coals.

Bent double he was, bent almost in agony to his knees, with a head that thundered, but pain by pain and fright by fright he forced his body straight and up into the open.

All he could foresee was the hangman.

All he could feel was a red and hot and blinding anger against Custard.

He wrenched the boy to his feet and dragged him like an animal on a rope.

"Fool."

Custard went with him, sobbing.

"Shut your mouth. One more sound and I'll flatten you."

Back up the hill strode Prospector Tom, dragging Custard.

"I've lost my horse! I ought to strangle you."

Custard reeled on, pulled, wrenched, dragged, even after he had fallen.

He cried out, "You're hurting me."

But there was the little grey horse and Custard was pitched bodily across, to lie face down as if unconscious, across packs and pots and pans and shovels and a Bible in a box as big as a paving stone, where everything was so hot to the touch that heat struck back like irons through his clothing.

Prospector Tom grasped the reins and ran, groaning terribly, everything swaying and clattering.

chapter ten

THREE CHEERS BECAUSE HE'S DEAD

THERE WAS A DEEP overhanging of rock that became a crag where it met with the sky. Other things were there, like gigantic sculptures or huge creatures that had been caught unawares and turned to stone.

Noises were there as well, a rushing and thudding in among the rocks, as if invisible bulls were making an escape; a curious place indeed, Prospector Tom would have decided, if he had had the mind for observation.

He reeled into the shadow of the overhanging rock. The beautiful shadow, the shade, the relief, a place to fall down, a place of concealment, a place to rest.

Oh, the relief.

Little Horse at once changed into jelly, packs falling through him one by one, slipping and sliding through him, Custard sliding along with them, head first, and hard things and soft things and sharp things and blunt things tumbled everywhere about, liver and bones and kidney stones, all those mysterious things that made up the insides of a horse, but the ground held firm and there Custard stopped, while Prospector Tom and the leftover pieces of Little Horse went on making noises together, wheezings and gurglings, and Custard couldn't tell them apart.

Well, jolly good luck to them, he thought. May all their troubles be disasters. Terrible disasters would be wonderful. Fatal disasters would be perfect. And for a real happy end let 'em all die dead.

He groped up through the packs and pots and pans and shovels, surprised to find there were no gruesome bits of horse scattered about. The blood was his own (distressing, that), coming from scratches and gashes and wounds beyond counting, terribly serious, oh shockin', but he didn't wail much because Mum wasn't there to patch him up, so what was the point? And Prospector Tom was laid out on his back in a spread of ashes, his mouth wide open, the rest of him heaving like an ocean and sounding like water rushing down a pipe, his tall black hat having rolled off and turned on its top, looking like a tall black nest for a tall black crow on a chimney pot.

A proper shambles was Prospector Tom, heaving in the ashes, moaning in the muck.

So the morning wasn't a failure, all things considered.

Three hearty cheers, thought Custard, for that, then sighted Little Horse; a mound of horse, a mess, a kind of heap, as if made of brown jelly or soft wet soap.

Yes, thought Custard, pursuing the thought.

> Slippidy sloppidy horsey galloppidy,
> Slip at the bottom and slop at the toppidy,
> Slipple and slopple at front end and back of him,
> Horsey go sloppidy floppidy whoppidy.

Yes, thought Custard, a good day for some things. A song that's a real little ripper. But no one was around to hear it, not even Seth, who'd have thrust a hoe at him to shut him up, or a broom or a rake or a bucket or an axe. "Work to be done. Get on with it, kid. Let's see you hop."

Custard sniffed a couple of times and sobbed a couple of times and tried to say his song again, but it wouldn't come back, and that was a pest, because he was sure it had been *exceptional*.

Beautiful word that.

Exceptional.

Lor, I'm sore though. I feel awful. I reckon all me ribs is busted. And all that blood bleedin' out. All me strength bleedin' away, while Ole Tommy's lying there looking as if I could get up and go. I could, you know. He'd never catch up now, would he?

So Custard sat up straighter and rubbed hard at the tears and the sweat and dug a finger in his right ear and gave it a good twist because his head was making squeaking sounds. Well, he'd thought it was his head. He dug in his left ear then and gave that a good dig, but still could hear the squeaking sounds.

"Must be mice," said Custard, looking around.

Lor, it was a strange place. The oddest looking rocks he'd ever seen, some in the shadow, some in the sun, some as big as whales, some as big as dragons, some looking like gigantic wombats about to leap up and bellow, *Beware, beware, take care, gobble gobble*.

Well I never, thought Custard. And once they'd swallowed you, you'd turn into stone yourself. Glop. And you'd have granite for bones and basalt for blood and a brain of solid solid rock.

Just like Seth had always said he had.

All those savage rocks rampaging across the land, with a taste for everything that grew or breathed, snatching up humans and tearing down birds, drinking up rivers and stamping on trees, beating their chests, bellowing with rage.

Fee fie fo fum, we'll gobble you first and gobble you last and gobble you in between times, gobble gobble.

Help, thought Custard.

Rocks with heads and tails and eyes and mouths. I mean, I ask you. There they are. Rocks as big as dreams and dinosaurs. And everywhere a fella looked were noises that didn't make a sound, the ghosts of noises that had gone. Well, almost no sound. Just little squeakings. And all around were the ashes of fires and heaps of thrown-away bones and pictures in ochre of ponderous kangaroos with very large private parts painted on the overhanging stone. And Prospector Tom still lay dying by the twitch in the ashes and the mud.

Custard rolled his eyes and thought of words like oh dear and spear and ain't it awful queer round here, but didn't make a song of it just then. He thought of bull-roarers roaring and didgeridoos wailing and rhythm-sticks clacking and naked feet stamping, and everyone painted like skeletons in pale, pale clay, yelling, *We'll get you, we'll get you in the end.*

So he looked round again, very carefully, at the footprints and the mud. Footprints without boots and footprints with boots on!

I wonder, thought Custard, if I could walk home?

If I really hurried, do you think I'd get there? Trouble

is, I don't know which way to go. I bet Ole Tommy doesn't know either.

Don't see no trooper, thought Custard. Maybe he's deaf or something. Maybe I didn't yell loud enough. Maybe he didn't bring his ear trumpet. But I'll not be yellin' again until Ole Tommy's proper dead. That fella's hand's so big. That fella might as well have stuck me on an anvil and hit me with a hammer.

If you're goin' to die, thought Custard, stop twitching and get on with it.

You used to come to our house when you were Preacher Tom, your tall hat bobbling, and ruffle my hair, and pray for Bella to get strong, and for Seth to overcome the demon drink—though not when Seth was there—and be nice to my mum. Now you're horrible.

Up struggled Prospector Tom to prop on his elbows. He was grey and green and streaked with ashes and mud and gurgling most terribly.

The death rattles, thought Custard. So that's what they sound like! That's good.

"Me last breath," gurgled Prospector Tom, "has come. Into your care, Father God, I commit the spirit of me days. Oh, I do feel poorly, so near to snuffin' it. Forgive me for me shocking wickedness and open up the doors of Heaven and let me in. Amen. Amen."

Then he fell back in the ashes and the mud.

Hooray, thought Custard, he's dead.

chapter eleven

WASTELANDS OF HISTORY

A FEELING OF WELL-BEING came over Custard because Prospector Tom was dead, as if Mum had given him a nice plate of cinnamon bread and it was Sunday teatime, and Seth's turn to milk the cow again, which Mum insisted upon every now and then. "Because Custard's still a child, Seth, and I wish more for him than seven days' unceasing labour without rest." Being a kid had its moments, even if the moments didn't come often. So he drew a full breath, a bit like swallowing the prevailing wind, and was about to whistle through his fingers to call the trooper when he looked at the mud again. It had been nagging at him, because it was the kind of mud that went with real wet water.

And what rain, Custard asked himself, has there been since last September?

Whereupon, Prospector Tom struggled up for a second time and wobbled on his elbows.

"Father God," he said, "my dyin' plea I raise to Thee. Pardon my stupid sons and their stupid cousin Fred from the stupid crime of kidnapping this stupid kid, forcing me to rectify the situation by layin' down me sacred occupation and removing the visible signs of evidence from the scene of the crime. And while you're at it, I'd be much obliged if you'd lay a curse on the Soldiers of the Queen and confusion on the Lackeys of the Law and deliver me sons and their cousin Fred from the blood lust of Hangmen and Judges. And as a particular favour, why don't you visit some horrible plagues upon the Ruling Classes? Boils, maybe, or the galloping rots. May their crops be thorns and their children turn into bandits, like what me very own children turned into, the moment I wasn't looking."

And at once he collapsed into the mud.

I thought you were dead, thought Custard, but your speeches get longer. . . . And what's our goatskin doin' there all undone? Is that our very own water bag making gooey mud?

Prospector Tom rose for the third time and propped himself up.

"Father God," he said, "one last thing I bring to your attention. I was only doing what seemed right in the light of the time. I was only trying to be a protective father to me stupid sons and their stupid cousin Fred. And may the brave Rebecca know that I care for her dearly and would have loved to hang me hat on her hat rack, and I never meant no harm to her wretched little creature."

That's my mum, thought Custard, the cheek of him, and I'm the wretched little creature.

"Amen, amen," moaned Prospector Tom, and fell back again.

It must be like drowning, thought Custard. Up he comes and down he goes three times before you dig the hole and drop him in.

So he listened for sounds of the trooper, remembering those big boot marks; or maybe of the black fellows, re- membering the barefoot marks; but heard nothing but wind in the scrubland and the rattlings of the dead and the sigh- ings of the dying, and raised to his lips his two whistling fingers and applied them with such enormous vigour that his ears went numb and his nose bled and his throat was sore for several minutes.

Hurry, hurry, the whistle shrilled. This's the way to come. Here's the kid you should be finding. Custard the bustard, the flute, the spinach. Over this way where the rocks are gathered like tigers waiting for dinner.

Never seen rocks like them, I haven't, Custard went back to thinking. They're waitin' to grab me, I betcha, soon as I stop looking. Soon as this ole fella's dead beyond a question I'm loadin' up that pony and going home to my mum, though pickin' the right way to go's a bit of a prob- lem.

"Praise His name," said Prospector Tom, faint and dis- tant, from the flat position, "I hear no Benediction, I hear the trumpet call to awaken." And he sat up, swaying, look- ing like first thing in the morning.

That's terrible, thought Custard, have I been and gone and done it? Awakened the dead with me whistle, like me mum always said'd happen? Let's hope there ain't no deaduns lying buried there in the bushes a-waitin' for the resurrection.

He peered into the glare out there to check up on it and a pair of eyes peered straight back at him.

Gave him quite a turn.

Holy Moses, thought Custard. I mean *Holy Moses*. I mean Holy This and Holy That.

He peered again, and felt his heart go bump-bump-bump and his breath leap up fit to choke him.

Two eyes, all bloodshot and bleary, with whiskers all round them, peering right back at him!

A moment later there was *nothing*. Nothing but glare and stars in his eyes, popping.

Lor, thought Custard. Eyes with whiskers round the sides and underneath them.

Was it a white fellow or a black fellow or a hairy-nosed wombat? Or a real-live resurrected deadun woken up by his very own whistle?

"Amazing it is," said Prospector Tom, clearing his throat as if about to deliver an oration, "what the mortal frame can accomplish without folding in the middle. Thank you, Father God, for giving the strength to live to your dutiful servant Thomas, never the doubter, never the questioning apostle, and only the prodigal son when facing the most grievous an' horrible temptations, like gorgeous ladies and other things what we won't mention."

It's shocking, thought Custard, this fellow's alive and kicking, just like a brumby. I mustn't ever whistle again, never ever. It's terrible the things that happen. How many deaduns are there like him, out there lurking in the bushes? Thousands, I'll betcha, all the way back to Cain and Abel, sticking their bones together.

"Gimme my leg," says this fella to that fella, "and two

ears are enough for anybody, you greedy little grasper."

All because I blew me whistle!

"No pursuers to be heard," said Prospector Tom, an ear cocked to the distance. "Dodged them with distinction, but no thanks to you, little devil."

Wasn't hoping for the credit, thought Custard, dabbing at his nose, still bleeding from the whistle. Never wanted to dodge 'em, only wanted to find 'em, but that wasn't no pursuer I saw out there. It was a real live deadun.

"A sacred place I perceive," said Prospector Tom, swaying from his sitting position, but getting back his push little by little. "Signs and wonders all around us. Or is it the House of Satan to which you've brought us, little devil?"

I don't know, thought Custard, the things this fella calls me. It's a wonder I don't grow a fork in me tail and spike meself when I sit on it.

"Poor little grey horse," said Prospector Tom with feeling, "the pains and privations we suffer. Heat and cold and dust and desolation and the devious designs of the Devil. Through them all we come together. Patience, Little Horse, and in God's good time we'll come to the Elysian pastures of Heaven, but not yet for a season. First we find the Ophir, first we find the El Dorado, first we liberate the oppressed children of God's Kingdom."

I'm one of the oppressed children, thought Custard. I'm oppressed like an elephant was stepping on me.

"Aaaaaarrgh," bellowed Prospector Tom, leaping up like something gone crazy. "By the livin' Lord Harry and his legions of demons."

He sprang upon the goatskin and clutched it by the neck. "Good gawd almighty," he bellowed, "on a day like this, in a place like here, and how far forward and how far back to *sweet living water?*"

He threw up a hand over Custard that shook with terrible threat. "Doomed us to thirst you have. Doomed us to torment. Doomed us to madness and to death, little monster, little devil."

Up there shook the hand and Custard couldn't jump away from it or wriggle out from under it. Hadn't he tried running already? Wasn't everything the more terrible because of it?

But the hand fell away and the man slid to the earth looking older and sadder than all the sorrows of life could have made him.

"You're a curse on me," he moaned.

From side to side he moved his head. "That we should end like all the poor fools who perish in the wastelands of history, who die of broken heads or crazed spirits or madness from the thirst, who never get back to where the sea laps, who seek the Ophirs and the El Dorados but bleach their bones in the desert."

He fell silent.

After a while he said, "We could start back in the cool of the evening, but what would we see by moonlight? How would we find the water that only the sunlight can show us? And to travel in the sun is to die."

chapter twelve

THE TERRIBLE THINGS
THAT HAPPEN

"AMEN," said Prospector Tom.

Suppose it's my fault, thought Custard, it always is. If I hadn't run away we wouldn't be doomed to all these terrible things.

"Amen," said Prospector Tom, sounding very heavy.

But, thought Custard, if me father Adam hadn't got killed when I was a little boy, and me bully brother Seth hadn't gone to market that day, I wouldn't have got kidnapped, would I? Because Seth would have scrunched Jamie the captain and all his gang. Then I wouldn't have been here. And wouldn't have had to run away. And the water bag wouldn't have got busted. Like they say, what comes first, the egg or the chicken?

"I strike a bargain," said Prospector Tom.

So who's to blame for anything, thought Custard, since everything happens because some other fellow started it?

"I see a light upon the mountain," said Prospector Tom.

If I hadn't got born, thought Custard, they'd have been in a real pickle. Who'd they have blamed if they hadn't got me to shout at?

"Though perhaps I bargain with the Devil," said Prospector Tom. "Old Nick rules round this neck of the woods, I reckon. God wouldn't be seen owning it."

I ought to write a song about it, thought Custard.

"I hope you're listening to me," said Prospector Tom.

A real important song, thought Custard, like God Save the Queen, about everybody blaming the other fellow.

"Will you pay attention?" shouted Prospector Tom.

"Pay who?" said Custard.

"I'm talking to you," shouted Prospector Tom, "but it's like talking at a picket fence."

That was what Custard reckoned. Getting Ole Tommy to listen was practically impossible.

"You cut yourself a stick," shouted Prospector Tom. "You get yourself out there and busy yourself. You find some water or else."

"Or else?" said Custard.

"Or else we'll die," shouted Prospector Tom, "to begin with."

"I thought dyin' was the end of it," said Custard.

"Do as I say," shouted Prospector Tom, who had veins sticking out on his neck.

Oh, the suffering, thought Prospector Tom. This kid'll be me undoin'. He'd drive angels to drink. God knows what havoc he'd wreak in Heaven. What sort of day was it when God made him? Forgive me, Father God, for takin' such liberties, but I submit your concentration was strayin'.

I'm not goin' out there, thought Custard, with a stick in me hand, no jolly fear. I wouldn't go out there to save meself from drowning. I like it here in the shade. And who brung me in the first place? Is it my fault all the rivers and creeks and lakes and puddles are dried up?

"Get on with it," shouted Prospector Tom. "God stay me hand from violence or I'll kill the little beast."

I'm not gettin' on with anything out there, thought Custard. Spooks leaping at me out of holes. Spirits screechin' in the trees. Rocks turning into dragons. I'd rather die nice and peaceful of thirst.

"If," shouted Prospector Tom, "you don't shift your carcass by the time I count three, I'll beat the daylights out of you."

"I won't find water out there," wailed Custard.

"Why not?"

"I caaaarrrrn't."

"You'd better," bellowed Prospector Tom, "or they'll bury you in instalments."

"I don't wanna go out there," wailed Custard, "because there's a real live resurrected deadun with whiskers."

Prospector Tom's mouth fell open.

"Woke him up with me whistle, I did," wailed Custard. "A real horrible face I woke up. Eyes in the middle and whiskers all round."

"Come on, come on," said Prospector Tom, sounding cautious. "You don't expect me to believe that."

"I woke you up," wailed Custard, "with the very same whistle."

Prospector Tom thought about that, very seriously.

Grief, he thought, what a shockin' development. I *do* remember hearin' that whistle. And the brave Rebecca, her very self, doesn't she say that on Midsummer Eve and Halloween it's terrifying, and that on full moon nights no one in the house can sleep a wink, because this here kid gets lit up like a candle?

"Where'd you say you saw that deadun?"

"There," wailed Custard, "peerin' out of those bushes, and he wasn't no hairy-nosed wombat neither!"

Prospector Tom gave that some consideration also, and started rubbing at his eyes because he was seeing so badly. If he lived to be rich he'd be buying a nice pair of spectacles very first thing on the very first morning.

"No," he shouted, leaping up in anger. "I preach the Word of Freedom, not of Slavery and Superstition."

Out into the sunlight he stormed, stamping his feet and waving his arms, crashing through the bushes and raging round the rocks in a remarkable fever of motion, yelling at the top of his voice. Even as a boy he'd known that the more noise you made the better it was for the humans and the harder it was for spooks.

"Go away," shrieked Prospector Tom, rushing hither and thither and not staying in any one place long enough for a spook to get a hand on him. "Shoo. Shoo. Away you go, you spooks and demons and devils. I command you to get to Hell out of it!"

Goodness, thought Custard, what a performance.

Spooks scampering off in all directions there were. Custard saw them go. Saw the bending of the bushes and the swaying of the trees and the scattering of the leaves.

Back came Prospector Tom into the shadows, limping and coughing and sneezing from his extraordinary exertions.

"All right," he panted, "that's fixed it. Now get on with it."

"You don't think they'll come back again?" said Custard.

"Of course they won't."

"They'd better not," said Custard.

"Get on with it!"

Oh well, thought Custard, and crawled off.

"What are you crawling for?"

If those deaduns sneak back again, they'll think I'm a turtle.

"If I have to come after you," called Prospector Tom, "you'll be regretting it."

Shivers, thought Custard, talk about being between the Devil and the deep blue ocean.

"Cut the stick," bellowed Prospector Tom.

All me life dodgin' eyes in the bushes. Eyes and shapes and shadows and mists and things horrible, scraping their bones and rattling their chains and going *woo-oooo-ooooo* even after sun-up in the morning. I'll be blowing no more whistles, I'm tellin' you. I'll be thinking twice before I'll be blowing my nose even.

An' that rock dragon over there is growin' bigger by the minute. And that rotten old whale don't bear looking at. Poke him and he'd bellow, I betcha, worse than Ole Tommy.

"Get on with it," bellowed Prospector Tom.

It's like choosing between a shooting and a hanging, thought Custard. Which way's better when both ways are dead certain? There you are, dead lying down or dead swinging.

He started honing his knife, hissing and grimacing.

I ought to cut his throat with it, thought Custard, except that he wouldn't let me. That's the trouble when you're a kid and the other fellow's bigger than a cupboard. It's not decent livin' sixty years, I reckon. He ought to be a tombstone.

Here lies Tom Button, Dead as Mutton.

    Thomas Thomas Button Button,
    Dead as dead as mutton mutton,
    Deader deader yetteredder,
    Dead as I forgetteredder,
    Like me father Adam-daddum,
    Sleepin' in God's bosom-oosum,
    Ohhh rippy-dippy-oh,
    Ohhh rippy-dippy-ee,
    Dead him, dead him, dead-him-oh.

There's a likely-lookin' bush, anyway, thought Custard, everything considered, the heat and wind and that screamin' ole fella. A real nice little bush. Feels real friendly. Bend yourself this way and gimme that fork out of your middle.

He cut, hissing sideways, and stripped off the spidery flowers and the long thin leaves and trimmed up the ends and really liked the feel of it. Oh, very nice and friendly it was. Sometimes even pretty little bushes scratched back, slash, all of a sudden.

Now, thought Custard, you've gotta work real hard, little stick, like no little stick since they made you into a bush instead of a turnip. Think about that. You could have been a turnip and got eaten.

But finding water out here! I ask you! That's why deserts are deserts, innit? 'Cos the water's in the other places.

Always gettin' pushed. Everybody going push-push. Everybody wanting carriages to ride in and palaces to live in. Everybody wantin' to be rich. Everybody reckoning I'm the fella to find the treasure. Ain't even got myself a gut-bucket to play me a tune after supper.

I want to go home to me mum for a cuddle.

"Slow, slow," bellowed Prospector Tom, "slower than molasses."

I'm not slow. I'm a busy little bee buzzing in a bottle.

> Buzzy buzzie
> Buzzy buzzie
> Buzzy buzzie,
> Custard,
> Buzzy like a buzzie bee,
> Wuzzy buzzie fuzzy me,
> Buzzy muzzie duzzy me,
> Ever muzzy buzzily,
> Buzzy buzzie, buzzy buzzie, buzzy buzzie,
> Red hot mustard.

"I don't believe it," bellowed Prospector Tom, an inch from his ear.

"Yah," bellowed Custard, collapsing.

"Up," bellowed Prospector Tom, "or I'll flatten you flatter than a pancake, honest."

Up reeled Custard, shaking all over, and held out the stick again which shook along with him.

"What's it shaking for?" demanded Prospector Tom.

"Gug," choked Custard.

Once he was a nice old fella, thought Custard, and gave me barley sugar. Once he gave me a wind-up beetle. Now he gives me heart failure.

"What's it shaking for?" demanded Prospector Tom.

"Gug," said Custard, hair bristling like a halo.

"You're not answerin' me again," shouted Prospector Tom, "you horrible little creature."

Come on, stick, thought Custard, all of a quiver, you've gotta work real hard in a real big rush.

"What's happening?" demanded Prospector Tom.

Nothin'. Nothin'. Nothin'.

"If you don't find anything, kid, you know what'll be happening to you, don't you?"

I'll be dyin', thought Custard, all withered up and crackly, same as you.

Whereupon the stick flicked in Custard's hands and arrowed into the earth near his feet, as if he had sharpened its end like a dart and aimed it.

"Yah," he yelled, leaping back.

"You're not trying," bellowed Prospector Tom. "I've had enough of you. Enough of you with bells on. What'd you throw it for?"

"Yah," Custard went on yelling.

"Don't you understand," bellowed Prospector Tom, "that we've got to pull together or die of thirst?" He had Custard by the hair, holding on to a handful of it, and Custard was pulling like a fish.

"Pick it up!"

"I never did throw it," yelled Custard, turning frantic.

A hand like the wall of a house forced him down to the earth.

"Pick it up," bellowed Prospector Tom, beside himself with anger.

"I don't want to," cried Custard.

Up jerked Custard, yanked to his feet by his hair, and the stick was thrust into his hands and everywhere he looked Prospector Tom was there already.

"I didn't do it," Custard cried. "I don't like it here. Take me away from here."

Everywhere was awful, and there wasn't a corner left anywhere inside him to shelter from the world.

The stick was in his hands, its place found by habit, and he could hardly get his breath, not a proper healing breath of it, and every hair of his head stood up, separate and wilful.

"I'm frightened," he wailed.

The pressures in the stick, and the panic of it. The strength of it, that little stick thrusting.

Everything was turning fierce and foreign.

Everything was changing.

The stick arrowed back into the ground and he fled from it hysterically, seeing nothing, but Prospector Tom's arm grew behind him and stopped him with a jolt that jarred him to his teeth.

Shadows vanished and the hot inland wind felt dark and different, as if the world had become an oven of red-hot stones.

Black clouds were tumbling over the sun, clouds with

blazing gold edges, clouds black and blazing and thundering and tumbling.

"I didn't," wept Custard. "I couldn't. I wouldn't. I didn't ever do it. I didn't ever ever."

A hand with a weight like iron was pushing him down as if for praying, though in panic he kicked and yelled and squirmed against it, even though rain was crashing around them.

The terrible things that happen.

Oh, and all because of one little stick with a flower like a spider.

Up reared Little Horse whinnying.

"I love you," whinnied Little Horse, to the raining and the thundering. "You're sticking me together. I'm a horse with a whinny. You're gorgeous."

chapter thirteen

FIRST DAY OF RAIN
UPON THE PLAIN

"FATHER GOD," cried Prospector Tom to the wind and the rain and the storm, raising high one long arm, constraining Custard with the other, "how marvellous are your works. How miraculous are your messages."

All around were the ragings and the thunderings, and Custard in wildness of fright and spirit attacked at his side like a furious animal.

This caused Prospector Tom a lapse of appreciation.

"Though I confess, O Maker of All, that one of your minor works is a problem."

This was the appropriate moment to release Custard, and the boy burst from him, floundering and scrambling for the shelter of the rock, even though streams poured from its face and from the overhanging lip and made curtains through which he rushed.

"Oh shivers," sobbed Custard, throwing himself down, and was terrified of himself and didn't know where to hide from himself, or whether to scream and scream or beat his head on the ground. "I never did," he wailed. "How could I make a storm?"

"And a very good day to you," whinnied Little Horse.

"It's a change for the weather to be wetter, and the wetter the better, wouldn't you agree, little human?"

Up leapt Prospector Tom, his mouth like a gate in a wall to drink deeply of God's blessings, and did a modest skip, heels clipping, and made a sound, "Yeeee-eeeeee," which touched the edge of Custard's consciousness.

Out there the man had begun to skip with greater and greater vigour, clipping his heels sometimes twice before he hit ground.

"Boy, oh beautiful boy," he yodelled, "oh marvellous creature, it's a beautiful day to be alive, to be sure, to be certain."

Have I done somethin' right? thought Custard.

At which point Prospector Tom's dance became a jig, and he sang to the earth and the heavens and the in-between regions. "Oh my, oh me, oh miracles and marvels. A remarkable event has come upon the world this day, m'laddie, m'beauty."

I thought it was a disaster, thought Custard.

"Oh glory, oh-glee-oh, oh-merry-merry-merry-oh," yodelled Prospector Tom and danced across the open ground and through the streaming curtains and snatched Custard up and danced a circle with him.

"Hey," yelled Custard, "Hey, cut it out."

In legend and rhyme the day became known as the first day of rain upon the plain and the days that came later were numbered from it. Custard wrote songs about it, that were chanted by children as they played games. One was sung in churches for a hundred years for breaking droughts.

"My boy, my boy, my boy," yodelled Prospector Tom, "all is forgiven thee. Thy sins are washed away. Our God shows us the sign and points to us the road."

"The road to where?" wailed Custard.

"Fill the goatskin, my boy, catch God's blessings as they fall, sweet and pure and clean. Put out the dishes and wash your face and hands and your disgustin' little ears. Stack up the horse again and leave a place to ride, for you're going to ride in style."

"In the rain?" wailed Custard.

"Oh, for a cake of soap and a tub to lather in," yodelled Prospector Tom, "oh my, oh-me-oh," and tore off his clothes and went dancing through the streams that spilled from the face of the rock, yoo-hooing and leaping on long bony legs, while Custard stored up astonishments and did as he was told.

It was a beautiful cliff, it really was, sticking out up there, hanging out over, for keeping off the rain. Like a tent set up on the plain. Like having a house for a change.

We could light a little fire, thought Custard, and bake lots of bread and watch the storm crash down. It'll be gone soon, in an hour. Real marvellous bit of shelter. What's he want to leave it for? He can go off on his own and I'll wave goodbye. Ta-ta to you, Ole Tommy. And off he goes. Over the hills and far away. Over the hills and fall down a hole.

What's the water pourin' from the sky for, when the stick is stuck in the ground? Should be comin' up like a geyser, instead of thumping down all around.

"Here," said Prospector Tom, and picked him up like a

bag of bones and threw him on the horse, and tied a cord about his ankle while Custard watched surprised.

"Hey, what's this? What's this here?"

Prospector Tom looped the cord through the girth and knotted it twice and Custard couldn't move his foot more than an inch, and couldn't even bend down to untie it for fear of falling off on his head.

"Hey," said Custard, "what's this about?"

"No more tricks," said Prospector Tom. "I'm aimin' on keepin' you, kid."

"But what if I fall off?"

"Don't," said Prospector Tom.

"What if I slip?"

"You'll get dragged along by the foot," said Prospector Tom.

"Lordy," wailed Custard, "what about me head? I'll get me brains bashed out."

"What brains would they be?" said Prospector Tom.

"If I get me brains bashed out," wailed Custard, "I'll be a right proper nit."

So he clung on like a climbing bean. So he pressed in his knees and grabbed a handful of mane.

This terrible ole man, thought Custard, he's really really going out in the rain.

Thus was resumed the quest for the golden El Dorado on the first day of rain upon the plain.

"He's barmy," wailed Custard.

Silly Ole Tommy, away he went, striding on ahead, off through the dragons and the whales and the dinosaurs, all those great boulders, all those great rocks, marching off.

I dunno, thought Custard. Rain runnin' down me neck. Rain runnin' down me back. Rain runnin' down me tum. And Lordy, rain runnin' down to me you-know-what. And he forgot our lunch. I mean, he forgot to eat!

"Hey, I'm hungry," wailed Custard.

Plodding away went Ole Tommy, singing hymns, not even looking back.

"O for a thousand tongues to sing," sang Ole Tommy.

It'd make you sick, thought Custard. It'd make you real bilious. Horrible ole fella he is. How'd he live to get so old?

"Hey, I'm hungry! What about our lunch?"

Ploddin' away the ole fella went, water streamin' all around, plodding off like he knew where he was going. I'll bet he doesn't though, thought Custard. I'll bet you we get lost.

chapter fourteen

WESTWARD HO

THERE WAS BEDLAM in the rum shanties after she passed through.

"Gawd, there's a woman for you!"

"Yow-eeeee."

"Wouldn't I leave home for that!"

"You and the rest, mate!"

"All those years, they say, livin' in a mud hut. What a waste."

"And where would you be invitin' her, man? Home to your tree?"

Down behind the woodheaps there was talk among the kids, of a similar kind.

"Wow, did you see the lady? The lady on the horse? The lady with the gun? The lady with the dog? The lady who's the mother of the Golden Goose? Wow, I thought she'd be ugly as sin after what me auntie said to her friend."

There were declarations in the parlours and the summer kitchens.

"That *woman*," said the women, "is riding bareback. Is riding with a gun. I saw her with my own eyes sitting on a cart horse like a man."

"They say," said the women, "that the governor called on her every day."

Youths climbed trees ahead of her and dropped stones. One who scored a hit with a rock as big as his fist bragged about it for days.

"Nearly threw her, the horse did. Had her gun, too, but she didn't get me. All she got was leaves!"

At night Rebecca built two compact fires and rested between them. If the moon came up bright, if the country lay visible, she moved on, the butt of her musket tucked under her arm. Life felt less of a loss then.

"The land's outside my comprehending," she said, addressing herself. "I stand upon the mountains and can't see to an end. Yet there'll be no end unless I go to it and make it. If I turn a hundred ways, each way may take me a thousand miles, but only one way is the right way. Which way is that?"

Canyons, like great splits in the earth, as if about to split farther, lay below her. Endless, endless were the treetops. Troubled oceans of treetops were there, through which she had to pass. A million gnarled trees were there rooted among a million razor edges, and the softness of the blue distances was an illusion.

Columns of smoke billowed from distant ridges, great clouds of smoke of every evil colour, as great as great storm clouds, exploding into dark fire as if by some wicked whim or some demon's deadly touch.

Each day the fire was in another place. Each day smoke

billowed from somewhere else. In an instant, caught within it, she'd be ash.

Somewhere near here, she thought, my little one passed. I could step across his grave and hear nothing but winds and the shrieking of the heat.

There were bushrangers and fugitives and runaways in the mountains.

There were blacks.

Her fortress in the forest, built by Adam those long years before, was almost too far off.

The unanimous opinion in the rum shanties was that she was heading west.

"Well, it's the way the mob's gone, and the way the mob's stayed, because no one's come back."

The mob had been heading that way since the Preacher had gone through, round by the quiet ways, months back, along the gullies, skirting the cliffs, breaking his own track. There wasn't much the locals missed. Half of them lived in caves or hollow logs and were always on the lookout; half of them were watching for troopers night and day.

"Got the Golden Goose he has. And bein' a preacher and all! What do you know about that!"

"Load your little wheelbarrow, mate, and we'll be slinking along after and playin' the same game."

And away they'd gone, leaving their hollow logs behind.

> Sing Golden Goose,
> Sing Golden Goose,
> Sing Golden Goose, my hearty.

A gang of boys came through, bypassing the settlements, bypassing the shanties, bypassing the inns, sleeping under the stars, and looking guilty if you tried to get near. Then they'd run. But people watched them come and go, and locked their doors and barred their windows and let the dogs run loose, though every now and then a chicken would be gone or a bag of flour or half a row of carrots from the garden bed. It was handy having strangers to blame.

"But did you get an eyeful of the nose?" they said in the rum shanties.

"What a conk."

"It's that preachin' conk. It's the Preacher's little kiddies runnin' after their dad."

Every now and then some of the few left behind rolled their swags or loaded their wheelbarrows and went the same way; heading west, out through the mountains, down to the plain.

"Gold," they agreed, "is no laughing matter."

They oiled their guns or honed their knives or tried the weight of their shillelaghs and followed on after. Followed on after the Preacher, or followed on after his sons, or followed on after the mob, or followed on after they read the Proclamation bearing His Excellency's Command, or followed on after the woman who rode bareback, hair streaming black and long. By then most of them had gone.

In the parlours the women said, "She's shameless."

Down behind the woodheaps the kids said, "Let's cut ourselves a stick, hey, and have a try. If the Goose can do it, so can we. You know they say there's a price on him of two hundred pounds? As much as a proper house, my mum says, with glass windows and a slate roof. One kid worth two hundred pounds, not even dead or anything. *Alive!"*

All through the mountains and round the towns kids with sticks trod with high-stepping strides and wide bright eyes. Some struck water. Some fell down crab holes.

In the rum shanties the halt and the blind and the lame said, "That Preacher's in trouble, if you ask me, if he hasn't perished of the heat or the thirst."

"I'd be keepin' me head down if I was him, if he's not lyin' down dead with a spear in his ribs."

"If them bad men out there, you mean, haven't already done him in."

"They say she can shoot the smoke out of a man's eye at a hundred yards. Gawd, but I'd be goin' meself if I wasn't too frail to lift an arm. Fill up me glass again, Bert, if you don't mind."

A limb of the great fire of 1851 stood between Rebecca and the plain.

"Who can comprehend this country?" she said. "Who can *stand* it?"

It was 115 degrees in the gullies, 115 at least.

God alone knew what it was higher up, if anything still existed higher up. God alone knew where the main fire burned, for who could see it but God? God alone knew where it would appear next, for fires burned above the earth in the sky.

Tree branches burned up there, swirling in the up-currents. Billions of ribbons of bark and leaves and ferns and feathers and hair and flesh flew fragmented on the winds, flaming and falling and billowing up again.

The smells on the wind were the scorchings of death.

Rebecca edged the horse to a great tree, as great as ten feet through the butt, and shifted into the shifting lee of it, moving with the wind gusts.

"White Dog, sit!"

Up there in the sky, eucalyptus gases in clouds turned into flashes of fire as if huge lanterns flared on and off. Soot fell. Branches fell. Pieces of trees fell from high up.

Three men came, as if hurled from the edges of a spinning wheel, one on her left, one on her right, one appearing almost ahead.

She saw them through the smoke.

They ran with low hard strides, as if their strides were too long, as if their bodies were compressed by weights, as if their bodies soon must split, as if nothing propelled their bodies but a kind of witless striving.

"I am the Amazon," the brave Rebecca said, listening to herself. *"White Dog, sit!"*

The men ran past, one so close she could have called him.

Rough-clad men they were, bearing digging tools and cooking pots and blankets on their backs, faces darkened by sun and dirt and smoke.

They ran past and didn't know she was there.

"Poor creatures," she said.

White Dog cried softly.

The cart horse sweated and twitched and she held hard

on his reins and soothed him with words. "Good lad," she said. "Be calm. Be calm."

Thousands of birds flew past, some falling scorched from their flight, not looking like birds after they had fallen to the earth.

Snakes and huge lizards, lizards longer than her arm, fled deeper into the gullies from which she had come.

Creatures of the forest leapt past, as if flying on the ground, striking themselves senseless against rocks.

"Poor creatures," she said, and soothed her horse, stroking him. "Be calm. Be calm. *White Dog, sit!*"

The coming of the great fire was a noise beyond all comprehending, like everything else, yet she knew she would not run from it, that birds might fly from it and creatures might flee from it, but Rebecca was different.

"WHITE DOG, SIT."

She sat upon her horse, soothing him, stroking him. "Good lad. Good lad."

The flames in the gullies were red, shot through with black.

Black fire she saw in the gullies on three sides. Black fires in the gullies where the men had fled, and the lizards and the snakes, and all fried in their own fat.

"I'll die here," she said. "I expect."

Fire like gold flamed from the heights and only dragons could breathe the air. Dragons were up there, clearly in sight.

"Be calm, old friend, old horse. WHITE DOG, SIT!"

The first day of rain on the plain burst upon the mountains.

chapter fifteen

SLISH-SLOSH

SLISH-SLOSH WENT poor Custard far out upon the plain, so far away from home, and out in front there strode the man and all around the rain crashed down.

> Pitter patter,
> Patter splatter,
> Splatter splitter,
> Splitter shatter,
> Schlummmphhh,
> Went the rain.

Well, thought Custard, when you get as wet as me, you can't be writin' songs like Schubert or McPhee.

Who's McPhee?

Pouring, pouring, down it came, as in ancient times, thought Custard, when Noah built the ark, and the whole wide world became a sea and nothing else stayed afloat. Pouring, pouring down (when Noah built the boat) and all the bullies sank to the bottom making gluggling sounds. But the plucked pigeons like Custard walked aboard two by two, with the giraffes and the guinea pigs, and went a-sailin' into the sunlight, strumming on their gut-buckets and blowing their tin whistles and having a wonderful time.

Well, they must have done, thought Custard. Who'd

drown a kid like me and really really mean it? Though drowning people like Seth might have something to commend it.

Looking back from time to time was Custard, and looking elsewhere about, and sniffling and snuffling in the ever-lashin', ever-lastin', never-ending wet.

They're following me, he thought.

Things are following every step, some with bleary-looking eyes and whiskers and some with faces I wouldn't want to think about.

"Oh true," cried Prospector Tom on the second day of rain upon the plain, gales beating at his chest, rain scudding round his head, his tall black hat jammed down so hard his ears were bruised and red. "It's the omen, I say, for eyes to see and ears to hear and mouths to shout about. The omen to mark the end of a wicked, wicked age."

Slish-slosh went poor Custard, but at least he got to ride even though his leg was tied. Seated on the pony, slish-sloshing through the wet, while Prospector Tom strode on ahead, and all around were presences and feelings and sighings and pantings and *goodness knows what*.

Yet nothing moved upon the plain that Custard could clearly see, except endless driving gloom. And nothing blew upon the plain but winds of bitter cold or swirling rain, depending on the day, depending on the mood.

> Summer autumn winter spring?
> No one knows so ask the king,
> Or the queen if she's around,
> Dead's the king and in the ground.

Allay-allay-loo-yah,
Me bum is numb.

Poor ole king he's buried low,
Down where all the good kings go,
She's the queen when he fell dead,
So I'm told or so it's said.

Allay-allay-loo-yah,
Me bum is numb.

Tell her make it nice an' fine,
Tell her that the sun should shine,
Not the wet and not the cold,
Not like Noah's days of old.

Allay-allay-loo-yah,
Me bum is numb.

Don't she know I want it dry?
Oolie goolie pickle pie.
Auter wintum springer sum?
Tweedle-dee or Tweedle-dum?

Allay-allay-loo-yah,
Me bum is numb.

There were other verses, lots and lots.

"Ah, yes," cried Prospector Tom on the third day of rain upon the plain, "God says the world is washed of dirt and cleansed of slime and soon a bright new sun will shine on hills of burnished gold."

Well, let's hope so, thought Custard, because I've had enough of this sloshin' to and fro, because where we're going no one knows and when we get there who'll tell us we've arrived?

"Cut the sticks, boy," he keeps on shouting, but don't he hear what it's sayin'? Every time I cut a stick the harder pours the rain!

Looking back was Custard, and everywhere about. Night and day he had the twitch, day and night the same.

"God shows the sign," shouted Prospector Tom on the fourth day upon the plain. "Praise His Name." But his voice was sounding thin by then, and defiant by then, like a bird on a steeple in a high wind.

But plodding on he was, still out in front, water pouring all around.

"The old world goes washing down the ditch," he shouted. "See it go a-swirling and a-sinking. A new world will rise with ivory towers in the rain-washed sun and we'll drive our carriages on streets of gold."

Slish-slosh, thought Custard, slopping back and forth on the wallowing little horse, if we don't turn into ducks or tortoises first, if we don't get the galloping mildews, if we don't go glugging down the plughole into the middle of the earth. I wish he'd send me back to me own little house, back to me mum and back to Bella, back to Seth me bully brother. Back to his nagging and screaming.

"Time to bring the cow up, kid. Feed the horses. Fetch the bucket. Chop the wood."

Well, thought Custard, nothing's perfect.

"Gold," yelled Prospector Tom on the fifth day of rain upon the plain, "buys freedom for my stupid sons. The sons of Preacher Tom, reared with tender loving care to glorify the Lord. It's the poor what get hung in this stinkin' land, but if I'm filthy rich meself who'd dare, who'd dare, *who'd dare?"*

Slish-slosh, thought Custard, his thoughts sloshing round through the water in his head. Nothin's left in me noggin but a muddle-puddle. If you listen you can hear it slish-sloshing round. Through one ear water pouring in, and out the other there they run, uggle-gluggle down the drains, go me silly-lookin' brains.

"Lor," cried Prospector Tom on the sixth day of rain upon the plain. "It's wet."

chapter sixteen

CATS ON COALS

DANCING BACK and forth they were, like cats on coals, though there wasn't a cat or a coal this side of *make a fortune and settle down at home and put your feet up, me hearties, and toast your twinklin' toes in front of the precious flame.*

This was a view voiced among the mob coming along in the rough behind.

"Round and round he goes," they cried, "this crazy Preacher man.

"Excusin' us the liberty, lads, of criticising the respected family name, but this old man of yours is driving us all to drink faster than the rigours of the rain.

"Round and round we go like maypole time in England o'er the main, where we'll not be dancing for a time, if ever, in view of sundry matters not for recollecting out loud in front of kids like you brung up so refined.

"But getting out of this ole coot's way is harder than chasing him through the rain, again excusin' us the liberty, lads, of criticising the founder of the family fame.

"Why don't he take his blinkers off? Why don't he open his eyes, at least to blaze his trail by chippin' at the trees?

Don't he see he's been through here every other day for longer than a sentence in your local friendly jail? Every time he clears his throat he turns himself around and starts heading off across the ground where his footsteps scarce have washed away, from passing by the other day.

"Here he comes again," they yelled. "My gawd, my gawd, and coming like a train.

"There'll be a song about it, my hearties, for singing in the rain:

Here he comes and thar he blows and here he comes again,
Round and round and round like Muvver Murphy's crinoline.

"And the crinoline, me friends, what can circumfercate the lady of our song, is the most tremendous hoop, widely be it known."

But not a note was sung in days.

No one lit a cooking fire.

No one stewed a bone.

No one had a decent feed or went hunting native game.

No one started up the song they especially sang that year:

Sing Golden Goose,
Sing Golden Goose,
Sing Golden Goose, my hearty.

Not a verse was added, not a sound of it was heard as the rain crashed down, for who could say the Preacher man wouldn't suddenly appear like the wrath of God clapping worse than doom?

"Me sainted fathers gorn before," he'd bellow across the land, "they've followed me, the scum. The minute I digs the hole that shows the gorgeous gold they're gonna do me in and steal me little chum."

And he'd be not far wrong.

So hidden in the dark they were, pressed against the rocks, pressed against the trees, exhausted to the bone, sheltering from the rain and the raging of the wind, having miseries such as they had never had at home.

Chewing on jerked meat they were, real rugged stuff and horsey, and ship's biscuits that should've died at sea back in 1840, and berries from the wild that were wild as Bengal tigers.

"Take a rash bite on 'em, lads, be a moment careless, and off'll come your heads from straight across your shoulders, red and raw and hairless.

"Bald you'll be, I'm warnin', in most distressing fashion, from crunching on them berries and from the corroding effect of the constant pouring water, the senseless use o' which being the well-known cause o' baldness in the young and hearty, and the rusting up of essential organs in the frail and failin'.

"When I'm rich, young fella-me-lads, me hearties, I'm never going to submit me sacred skin to any kind o' water, and never going out no more in the rainy weather, which is putting the human body to the most inhuman suffering, for what it was not intended, for I've been watching 'em all me life, dying like flies around me, from committing the human structure, what was meant for terra firma, to the perils of the water."

"Here he comes again," they yelled.

Diving into the slush they went, praying for wheelbarrows to look like blobs, posing themselves like lumps of rock, shinning up the tree trunks and looking like possums or bats or cankers full of grubs, depending upon whether they hung right side up or upside down or clung to the boughs with desperate hugs.

"Silly old coot," they yelled, "can't he steer a straight line? Can't he pitch a camp and chuck his anchor out? Can't he wait till the weather gets fine?"

chapter seventeen

A COMPANY OF SOLDIERS

THE RIVER OUTSIDE TOWN ran thick and roaring and grey and yellow and brown, marbled with the ochres of the earth, splashed with a million spears of rain. Like a serpent in a chasm for the brave Rebecca to engage.

"All the earth is against me," she sighed, "every rock and stone."

Vegetation, uprooted and torn, charred in the great fires, came down from the black mountains on the flood, rolling and bobbing and swirling, building up in turbulent heaps at the foot-crossing and the ford, stabbed through with severed shafts of ancient fallen trees flushed from the forest floor. The heaps shook, stressed by wind and onrushing current and rain, always about to topple, always about to crash across the causeway.

Beyond the roaring flood the village cowered, the last village, for all she knew, between the mountains and the end of the world; vague and low and grey, hazed by spray springing from the rooftops, almost hammered into the earth by rain.

Beyond the flood not a human soul moved. Not a swirl of smoke or a glimmer of light showed. All looked as abandoned as a thousand years gone.

Well, she thought, it might as well be, for who'll be crossing to anyone there, or who'll be coming back to me? Yet I must knock at the barracks door. The soldiers must open it to the storm. There I must stand and shout like the rain.

"I am Rebecca of Inglewood. I have come to take my son home, as I have vowed. But I am one woman against men of malice and greed, against hooligans and deceivers and murderers and thieves, and against another who called himself Preacher and friend and betrayed my trust. He is not to be forgiven and he and his sons will pay a high price by my hand.

"I am but one woman and a dog and a gun against them all. That is not a fair match. I learn that out there the dregs of the earth gather between me and my son, for it is common talk among free men and no free man would venture there. This far I have come alone, but this day I demand a company of soldiers that I may go on. To that end I bear the governor's warrant."

She held her sad horse at the brink of the flood, his head low, rain streaming from him, as it streamed from every living and inanimate thing. She caressed him with her knees. She soothed him.

"Good lad," she said.

She called down to White Dog in the mud, "Be calm. All is well."

Rain beat upon her, as if to her skin. Her clothing clung heavy and chill. Her hair like wet rope fell dark and long, as if endless issues of water flowed from her head.

To come to this, she thought, is a terrible thing. But I have sworn the oath. I will find him and bring him home. Nothing may separate me from my son; no man, no fire, no flood.

"I will cross this river," she said. "They will open the door to me.

"White Dog," she called down. "Up!"

The wretched creature leapt from the mud and she snatched at fistfuls of fur and dragged him across her pack.

"Go," she said to the big horse, and clipped him with her heels. "It's only water. It's only mud. We're in your care, Father God. Bless those who have the courage."

The cart horse went on, his legs planted as if drawing a huge load to the crest of a high hill. Water buffeted at his breast. Heaps of debris tottered about him, and built again, lurching as if to fall, tearing apart as he passed, logs pitching in the flood like clubs wielded by gigantic men.

"Good lad," she said, and soothed his head, and urged him on, and on, and on, his legs like buttresses in the flood.

"Good lad," she said, "and thank you, Father God."

She rode into town along a roaring yellow street, sheets of clear water pouring from roofs, but underfoot ran torrents of mud.

The faces of children pressed at window panes; the faces of women also; even the faces of men were like pictures in frames.

Storekeepers stood in dark doorways and coals glowed

deep in blacksmiths' shops and anvils rang and from red-lit gloom travellers peered out, like the travellers she had seen with wheelbarrows, like the travellers she had seen consumed by fire as they ran.

"It couldn't be her," they said, as she passed. "She couldn't have come through the flood."

When she found it, the notice said *Depot. 14th Light Dragoons.*

She rode into the yard and hitched the horse under shelter and knocked twice at the office door with the heel of her gun.

The door opened. The soldier there squinted out and tucked his shirt in.

"Soldier," she said, "I wish to speak with the commanding officer."

"You'll be meaning me, ma'am. I think."

"Soldiers without rank are not commanding officers," she said.

"Round here they are, ma'am. Why don't you come in out of the rain and tell me about it?"

"I am Rebecca of Inglewood."

"I had a feeling you were."

"I bear the governor's warrant."

"I feared as much."

"I have come for a company of soldiers," she said.

"Lady, I'm a married man. I've got three kids."

"I have come for a company of soldiers," she said, "and I bear the governor's warrant."

He sighed. "The only company round here, ma'am, is

me and Trooper Dodge, the first soldiers you'll meet in a hundred miles, and the last you'll find this side of India. And he's out on his pension next year, ma'am. Those roughnecks out there are real bad men. There are hundreds of 'em."

"I demand a company of soldiers," she said, "to help bring back my son."

"Come in out of the rain, ma'am. Please. It's beating in somethin' dreadful. I'll catch me death."

chapter eighteen

THE BENEFACTOR

"NEVER IN ME LIFE have I seen the like of it," gloomed Prospector Tom, wringing out his socks and putting them back on again and beginning his oration of the evening of the sixth day.

"Rain all day," he gloomed, "and rain all night. Can't sit up bent, can't lie down straight, and me trousers feel like something I wouldn't want to mention."

Me very own feelings, thought Custard.

"Talk about the end of the world," gloomed Prospector Tom. "Talk about castles on the sand. Talk about matches that won't strike and biscuits gone sour and endless pourin' water and one cranky kid and one crazy man and complete and utter madness."

Yes, thought Custard.

"Our Father God has done us down," gloomed Prospector Tom, knees up to his chin, arms wrapped around, huddling under the shelter of a few leafy boughs. "He said he'd never drown the world again, that's what he said to Noah, havin' drowned it once so good and proper. So it's Old Nick who's arranged it, curse his breeches and his bristles."

And there's nothing that can't get worse, thought Custard. Try waiting till tomorrow, me mum always reckons.

"Can't light a little fire," gloomed Prospector Tom, "to bake us a loaf or boil us a pot of tea and all around us is the everlasting roaring of the never-ending water."

Me belly button's sunk so far, thought Custard, that it's stickin' out the back of me.

"Or," gloomed Prospector Tom, "it's God's judgement on us for being so dog-wicked."

You speak for yourself, thought Custard.

"Child of Satan," gloomed Prospector Tom, glowering. "Little Nick, I call you. You and your tricks. You and your sticks."

> Starvation, fire or flood,
> Or gluggle deep in mud,
> If someone falls down thud,
> Or spills a drop of blood,
> Who cops the final blame
> With the undying fame,
> No prizes for the game
> Of guessin' right his name?

And that's the solemn truth, thought Custard.

"Fallen I have," gloomed Prospector Tom, "from me former state of Grace, lured by the evil of your repute, thinking some earthly good could come of it. Preacher, they called me, and touched their caps as I went riding past, blessing them in their sorrows and preaching blood and guts for the uplifting of their spirits. Here he comes, the children chanted, here's our Preacher Tom. Tell us a story, Preacher Tom, of sinners burning up in Hellfire and Damnation, while our mum bakes a cake with caraway seeds and butter and puts the kettle on. Now I hide me face in a desert place, in disgrace, and Little Nick on me little horse sits as silent as the Sphinx, like there's never a word he's ever going to utter."

I talk in me sleep, thought Custard.

"The crown I would've worn in Heaven is struck out from God's accounting," gloomed Prospector Tom, "for I have sought the treasures of Earth and the gates of Hell have opened up and dumped oceans on me head."

It's a fact, thought Custard.

"And what gold has Little Nick brought me to make up for me crown in Heaven? If I had enough to pay off the Queen's bullies and build a little chapel with a steep-pitched roof and a tall bell-tower, there might have been something in it. A nice little chapel to retire in, with a black notice board and bright letters on it:

God's House
Everybody Welcome
Sundays at 11 and 3 and 7
Resident Pastor
Thomas Button.

But all I've got is an ache in me back and three busted shovels and two broken picks and a string of holes from here to Back o' Blitheration full of muddy water."

Pity he didn't drown himself in them, thought Custard.

"The Buttons are doomed to extinction," gloomed Prospector Tom. "Survived I have these forty years since the terrors of transportation, for an exceeding trifling matter, and built meself a nice new reputation. Survived all, to see me sons hung from a gibbet as long as a judge's jawbone, with meself strung up in the middle. They always said gold turns men into idiots."

Though the Buttons were runnin' at a gallop at the start, thought Custard.

"They're too dead stupid, those sons o' mine, not to be caught," gloomed Prospector Tom. "Haven't I always caught them at everything? And the Queen's bullies are real smart at catching the fools who run for it. And the ones they miss perish ragin' of thirst in the wild red yonder, all parchment-like and horrible."

Water water everywhere, thought Custard. Does he want it wetter?

"Gasping I am," gloomed Prospector Tom, "for want of a beauteous roast o' beef with crisp potatoes on it, and Yorkshire pud and sprouts and thick brown gravy and lashings of horseradish sauce and maybe a dash of mustard. If I don't get a square meal soon I'll be eating Little Horse, hoofs and feathers."

What'll I ride on then? thought Custard.

"You'll be walking," gloomed Prospector Tom, "on your own two feet, like the rest of us."

I thought I only thunk that, thought Custard.

Up the man leapt, shaking a soggy boot at the Heavens. "Whatcha rubbing me nose in the mud for? Devoted and faithful servant I've been all these long and terrible years."

Goodness, thought Custard.

"A hundred days in the wilderness is full an' plenty," shouted Prospector Tom. "All me suffering and privation and nothing coming down from Heaven but endless pouring water. And me sons getting hung, sure as the Day of Judgement, them not havin' the brains to button up their own breeches. Inheriting nothing from me but me nose, sticking out in front of them like a signpost. What a humiliation. Me noble nose stuck to the front of a mass of stupid people."

"Well, let's go home," said Custard. "I don't think it's much good here either."

"Good gawd," said Prospector Tom, "did I hear a human voice addressing me? Did something human open up its little trap and flap it?"

"Let's go home," said Custard.

"It talks," said Prospector Tom, "but let's go home, it says. Perish me for a porker, I couldn't pick east from west or me forelock from me kneecap. We haven't sighted sky in a week, and not in a hundred days a human habitation."

And him sneakin' round the back way, thought Custard, every time there's a chance of it.

"We can't go home," cried Prospector Tom, "till I'm filthy rich, but I'm gettin' poorer by the minute. And there's nothin' left in the larder but half a bag of flour and half a pound of salt. Boots all wore out and nothing left to mend 'em with. Clothes all tore and nothing left to patch 'em with. Rotting, I am, like a mouldy apple, from me toenails to me top hat. Mildew, sproutin' from me whiskers.

"I always reckoned God blessed me ministrations and took care of me kids while I was riding round the colony attending to His holy business. But up they get, the silly beggars, and tear me world down in a crashin' heap of rubble. And all I ever asked for meself was to be the fella to discover the gold that said *go suck eggs* to the ruling classes.

"I wanted 'em all to shout, 'God bless old Tom Button. He put gold in our pockets and bread on our tables and beauteous roasts of beef to feast on each Sunday.' But me vanity is me undoing. *Thou art a man,* God says to me, *I, thy God, am the Benefactor.*"

Whereupon, Prospector Tom wept.

My goodness, thought Custard.

Goodness gracious me, thought Custard.

He's hungry, thought Custard. Starvin' to death, poor ole fella. You never know your luck, he might be dead by morning, then he won't eat Little Horse and I can go on riding.

Munching leaves was Little Horse, on through the night as usual, munching quietly through the leafy shelter.

Still munching in the morning was Little Horse and looking all a-sparkling and a-shining and sleek and horsey, and bright on the horizon was a brand new sun, as gold as a sovereign, though bigger.

Oh, so big, so big, was the bright golden morning.

chapter nineteen

BRIGHT GOLDEN MORNING

UP JUMPED Prospector Tom.

Woops!

"Oh, my loving Father in Heaven. Oh, hallelujah, and look what's happened to the weather! Oh, sweet Custard, gather up the sticks and make up the fire. Oh, stir your stumps, it's the gorgeous dawning of the Golden Age."

"Ug," said Custard, groping up through the hazes and the mazes to where this remarkable thing was happening. Blue was up there, as if seen through rose-coloured glasses, and heat was up there as if about to drop like a sheet.

"Oh gorgeous, gorgeous," shouted Prospector Tom, leaping about in extraordinary fashion, "not a cloud do I see. Nothing but the mists of the Golden Morning. Nothing but the glowing and the gleaming and the steaming of the glorious Heavens. God rests from his rubbing and his scrubbing and ushers in the dawning of the bright new morning."

Or the devil's plumb piddled out, thought Custard.

"Busy, boy, busy," shouted Prospector Tom. "Nice dead sticks and nice dead grass and we'll burn it bright if it takes us an hour to kindle it, and I'll bake us a loaf and brew us a jug and it's a feast we'll have this morning."

Away stumbled Custard, paddling through the puddles and groping through the vapours that were swirling up from the earth like a great resurrection, everything a-steaming and a-misting. Snapping off dead twigs was Custard and breaking off dead branches was Custard, and Prospector Tom was yodelling and yoo-hooing and unrolling his bundles and laying out his dishes and rubbing the mould off them and polishing the rust off them and waving his wooden spoon and yelling to the throne of Heaven,

"Glory to God on High,
He's heard my fainting cry.
Yippee-ie,
Yippee-eeee,
Yippee yippee yippee.

"Oh my goodness gorgeous," sang Prospector Tom, "it's a rhyme I've done, without even trying, like King David in his cave, a-psalming and a-crying."

"Has he struck it?" came a yell from the vapours.

Custard missed his step and his bundle of sticks went spilling.

"Ay?" he said, his lip curling, his hair bristling.

"Do I hear voices?" asked Prospector Tom, only a voice himself, nothing of him being anywhere visible. "Do you hear voices?"

"Arrr," said Custard, looking for somewhere to hide, though not being sure what he should be hiding from, the voices or from Prospector Tom, it being much too early in the morning for important decisions.

"What's happenin' there, Little Nick?" demanded Prospector Tom. "Are you pullin' your tricks again?"

Lor, thought Custard.

The murmurings were all around, muffled and eerie and shapeless, nothing settling into human form, nothing looking like Little Horse either, munching on the shelter, where a fellow might wriggle safely into the earth like a worm.

"Arrr," he cried, turning wildly round, words welling up. *"Where are you, Preacher Tom?"*

Off blundered Custard through tussocks and scrub, through spurs and prickles and spikes and mud, and crashed into arms that hugged him round.

"Quiet," said the arms, so huge and strong, and panting into their closeness was Custard, panting into the closeness of Preacher Tom.

"We've been and gorn and done it, I fear. Camped in the middle of a settlement."

An alarming thought that was, even for Custard, and he started burrowing deeper.

"That won't do, boy," said Preacher Tom. "Stand up like the brave young fella who fought my very own wicked sons."

That's me he's talking about, thought Custard. I stood up in the middle of the paddock and fought 'em with me whip. *Crack!*

On his feet was Custard, looking back up.

You used to come to our gate, thought Custard, and I'd run to meet you.

"You're my eyes, boy, and my ears, for me hearing's not what it was and me seeing's a calamity."

The mists and the mysteries of the bright golden morning swirled about them.

chapter twenty

THE HUMAN FUNGUS

SILENT WERE the mists and the vapours moving through the desert.

Silent was the sun, somewhere rising, somewhere sinking, somewhere still beneath the sea, that being the nature of the gorgeous golden ball put there by God to separate night from day and to dry up the puddles and to make the rain and fog.

Silent was the globe of the world, rushing on through the heavens, hurtling into time, leaving no wake that anyone could see, except Custard, who saw it clearly in his mind. Oh, a gorgeous wake like peacock feathers and sea foam.

"I heard them," growled Preacher Tom, growling low like an animal in a corner.

"I heard them, too," said Custard.

"Shhhh," said Preacher Tom.

Munching on everything green and handy was Little Horse, a disgusting exhibition of gluttony and lack of proper appreciation of the seriousness of the situation, crunching and munching and blurting from both ends.

"Shhhh," hissed Preacher Tom, "you greedy little horse."

It's her tum turning over, thought Custard, turning all that green stuff into upstandin' grey horse. But my tum's worse, from having nothin' in it but digestive juices digesting me tum.

Silent was the earth, except for squelching sounds and squashing sounds and Preacher Tom taking off his tall black hat, scratching, and putting the hat back on.

"Dead quiet," he hissed, "though I guess it ought to be, boy, in a proper balanced universe, Sydney Town bein' but a memory, and all the inns shut, and no fishwives being in evidence this side of Billingsgate, thank the Lord for that. We're gettin' the bush disease, boy. First you hear the voices. Next you see the little men."

I've had that disease all me life, thought Custard.

Poised was Prospector Tom, like someone waiting for something to go bang.

But so silent it was, except for Little Horse belching and little streams trickling and sunlight rustling making fan shapes in the fog, as beautiful as Heaven ever was.

Waking up in Heaven in the morning mightn't be all that bad, thought Custard. Peeling the sunbeams from off your bed of swansdown, lifting your head from your pillow of soft night, having a breakfast of gorgeous pancakes and honey and omelettes light as flannel flowers, and bacon from the choicest hog.

Straining his ears was Custard.

"I don't hear nothin'," he said.

"Same here," said Preacher Tom. "Boy, I'm thinkin' we've got the rattles. I'm thinking we need to fill our bellies up.

Bring that wood in and we'll do somethin' about making us a banquet. I mean to say, who'd be way out here except the mad people and all the mad people are locked up."

"Hey, Preacher, whatcha gone quiet for? Weighin' up your gold dust?"

"Oh my gawd," said Preacher Tom. "Did you hear that?"

Real plain, thought Custard.

"Hey, Preacher, have you struck it rich?"

"What a shockin' turn of events," groaned Preacher Tom. "The beggars are there, all right, and we're propped up in the middle of the street, I bet."

"You're caught with the loot, Preacher, the real hangin' loot, so you'll be sharin' it or swingin' by one skinny neck."

"You hear what they're callin' me, boy? How would they know that? By which name I gave 'em sustenance, even the pennies from me pocket and the flour from me swag. Biting the hand that feeds it is a perversity of the human spirit."

"You started your prayin' yet, Preacher?"

"Lordie," said Preacher Tom.

"Gawd up in 'eaven, you should be sayin', Preacher, save me from me sins most foul what's finally bowled me out. Save me from the hangman's rope. Save me from this 'ere reward money the governor's offering for the bringin' in of the Preacher and the Goose."

Shouts of approval came from all about.

"My gawd," said Preacher Tom. "How many are there? And where have I got myself? And what's this here goose? What sort of goose, for gawd's sake? Boy, tell 'em. Tell 'em I snatched you from the jaws of death. *No, no,* you'll have to swear it was me own wicked plot to carry you off, or I'll be puttin' the rope round the necks of me darlin' boys who were born so stupid, inheriting only me name and me nose, and everything else from their mother, poor little brutes."

He leapt upon his pack, upon his pots and his pans and his bits and his Bible in the box, and rolled them up in a scramble, ends sticking out.

"I'm moving, boy. I'm running. I bequeath to you me little horse. God spare you from harm and hurt."

Out into the mist fled the preacher clutching his swag to his chest.

"It's meself," he wailed, "running like a rabbit and on a golden morning like this."

Well, thought Custard, I see it this way, I think.

Thinking about it in a half-second flat. Thinking it through quick as a blink.

By which time Custard had drawn his little knife and slashed through Little Horse's halter and was heading out after Ole Tommy before he vanished in the mist.

"Wait for me," shrieked Custard.

"Lordie," panted Preacher Tom, "and the evidence comes rushing after me like it was pinned to me coat."

"I'm comin'," shrieked Custard.

"There ain't no doubt of that," panted Preacher Tom, "and how did I get meself into it? One day preachin' the Gospel. The next drownin' in the soup. Let it be a warning. Kids clutter up the house something awful and bring you grief."

Scuttling on he went, long arms wrapped round his swag,

splashing through the scrub and the mud and the steaming of the puddles, Custard stretching out from his coattails, Little Horse on the rein stretched out behind that, everything clattering like a kitchen.

"Sprung up like toadstools they have," panted Preacher Tom. "Human *fungus,* I call 'em."

He was making noises now from the effort, hurting in his chest and grating out his words, because he had never learnt how to keep his mouth shut.

"All these years a-ministering to His flock. All these years seeking the lost lambs."

Straight into the barrel of a musket strode Preacher Tom, Custard still coming after, Little Horse coming after Custard, the musket going off in the middle like a great door slamming shut.

Caught up in some kind of agony was Preacher Tom, sliding past, going somewhere, touching Custard as he passed. And breaking all around were the shocking reverberations of the shot.

Seconds were tucked away in there that lasted a long, long time.

Very close was Preacher Tom, but already far distant on his journey, and little bits of things that had travelled the miles and the years with him were appearing in the air as if conjured up by a magician and were alighting silently on the ground.

There lay the man among the pots and the pans and the funny little bundles, astonished, as if about to shout at Custard, "Stop this thing." But there wasn't any voice.

There should have been an oration to celebrate the event.

"Father God, into Thy hands I commend my spirit, but let me thunder Hellfire and Damnation one last time."

"He's gone," Custard screamed, and saw a man drop a musket as if it had turned red-hot.

There fell a musket, falling, to lie among the pots and pans, to fall beside a tall black hat.

From Custard came a cry like a cat, and he leapt upon the man, screaming and clawing, savaging him, and the man dropped, shocked, howling for his eyes.

Custard ran into the misty wilderness of the bright golden morning.

He ran up and down and round and round and in straight lines, screaming, and at last fell down and cried.

He had been wishing his man dead, and it had happened.

"I didn't mean it," Custard cried. "It was only a game."

chapter twenty-one

FOSSIL REMAINS OF PREHISTORIC MAN

CUSTARD WAS LYING in a pool somewhere, as if resting between worlds, but a bottomless well was underneath.

Whooooooo, Custard thought, if I let go I'm gone, tumble, rumble, over me bumble, down and down into the middle of the earth.

Preacher Tom went through here, poor ole fella. Fancy having to go into the dark on his own. Down this way, through this hole, down and down, rumble and tumble, down and down.

I wonder what's below, as pitchin' through you go?

The boatman bending his back and rowing you over, singing as he goes.

> Hey-dee-ho,
> Row, row, row,
> Over the Styx
> And away we go.
>
> Ho, ho, ho,
> Who's gone below,
> Below he go,
> To woe, woe, woe.

Yippee-ie-ie,
Yippee-ie-oh,
So a hey,
And a hey,
And a hey-dee-ho.

Well, no good bein' glum about it.

I hope there's breakfast for my ole fella when they row him over and he arrives.

Noises started getting through to Custard from the world he had left behind; voices in the fog.

He stopped breathing.

No more breathin' today. I give it away. I go away with Preacher Tom because I stop breathin' today.

This is the way to go, thought Custard. You stop beating, Heart.

I hope that ole fella's not eaten all the breakfast. He should've known I wouldn't let him go on his own.

As soon as I arrive I'll have a couple of fried eggs and a nice lump of ham, straight off his plate.

I'll die in a minute and here I'll lie like a schlomp on the ground.

"That's not the kid," they'll say, looking at the schlomp. And off they'll go.

Or I'll turn into stone and when someone digs me up in a million years, they'll say, "These are the fossil remains of prehistoric man. Note the remarkable brain. Much larger than a pea, despite what its brother Seth used to say in moments of jumping up and down in rage. And pray observe, fellow digger-uppers, the creature's name etched upon the stone:

"*Custard, the bustard, the singer, the flute.*"

Well, it'd better be, by jiminy, I want to be more than just a crummy ole bone.

His heart was still going clang, clang, clang, like a church bell across the plain. Cross about that was Custard. Oh, *very* cross. And he couldn't keep his breath out for another second.

Grrrrr, thought Custard.

He was getting dizzy for need of air. He was getting a pain. So he took a huge gulp and went clawing up through the mud, scratching at his hair.

"I dunno," he grumbled. "Honest I don't. Other people die real easy."

A desert of steam it was, waiting for him out there, billowing all around.

Stupid, thought Custard. First it's all hot and horrible. Then it's all wet and horrible. Now it's on the boil.

All on me own, I am. That ole fella's gone. I'm never going to have another dad. I can't stand the strain of havin' them killed all the time. What did they want to go and shoot him for? He knew more stories than my mum and told them better besides.

Custard sniffed.

It was nice hearin' his stories while bread baked in the coals. It was nice eating the bread. Had some real good words he did. Even rolled his rrrr's. Dancing round they went, trilling like birds. I can't roll my rrrr's.

Searchers were crashing through rivers of steam and

valleys of steam and hills of steam, as if the steam were being smashed to pieces by rampaging boys. But the soft world kept coming back to hide him, as if rising from a sea.

That's a pretty idea, thought Custard.

Rainbows were in the air, big rainbows in the steam, and little rainbows were dripping from twig-ends to splash upon the ground.

That's pretty, too, thought Custard.

But the heat was like a bakehouse. Perhaps the steam would melt and there poor Custard would be for everyone to see, stuck in the mud like an old boot, for the scalawags to rush upon, all yelling, "He's mine. Give him to me."

They'd start murdering each other then, in a struggling heap of limbs, like a bunch of caterpillars fallen from a tree, and the one left over would grab Custard by the neck and rattle him. "Right you are, kid," he'd say, "you're mine. Lead me to the gold."

That red sun up there was looking huge, was looking hotter all the time, so Custard started piecing the shouting together, thinking it was time, the shouts he should have heard before and the shouts that were happening still.

"This fella's dead, I reckon. Dead as they come. Dead as they go."

"Oh Gord in his Heaven and the devil below."

"Who's dead? What's that they're sayin'?"

"Where'd the kid go? Who saw the kid run?"

"Who fired the shot? What's the shot mean?"

"He's scratched me eyes out, the fiend."

"Custard, do you hear me there? Custard, come over here."

Come over where, thought Custard; who's callin' my name?

There were wails and cries. "Is my dad dead? Is that what they're sayin'?"

"Is he dead? Is that what they're sayin'?"

"Our dad's dead, they're sayin'."

"My dad," someone cried, high and shrill, "my dad can't die."

Custard frowned in his mud puddle. Whose dad were they talking about now?

"Why don't someone catch the kid? How could the little perisher get away?"

"It's the kid that's dead, they say."

"Gorrrrr love us. Who killed the kid? I'll kill the fool."

Am I dead? thought Custard. I didn't feel it happen.

A shadow passed yards from his head, mumbling and stumbling and swearing. Real bright language it was.

"What fool fired the gun?"

"Hell's fires, who says the kid's dead?"

"My dad my dad my dad's dead."

"Gawd, is everybody dead?"

"I couldn't help it, mate. I never meant to harm the old bloke. He's scratched me eyes out, the little fiend."

"Whose eyes?"

"My eyes."

"Who's the fiend?"

"Swipe me, they've gorn and killed the Goose."

That sounds interesting, thought Custard. I hope they roast him with potatoes. I hope I get invited.

"If the kid's dead, someone'll walk the plank. I'll push 'em off meself."

Me heart, thought Custard, is going like a forge.

"Whatcha want to kill me dad for? I'll kill you, I'll kill you back again."

"Oh, lemme go. Me eyes are full o' blood and tears."

"He killed our dad he did."

Lor, thought Custard, all this deadin' and dyin'.

"I'll kill him. I'll kill him. I'll kill him."

There they go again, thought Custard. Everybody killing everybody. There'll be no one left but me.

Going reflective, was Custard.

Yeh, he thought, Preacher Tom had lots of sons, as well I know. Ho ho, do I ever. But for them I'd be at home, hoein' the row.

There was Jamie Boy, the captain, the general, the boss of us all. And Kenrick van der Mellow Mere, who had pimples on his noble Roman nose, and everywhere else I reckon, from what I saw. And Hector the lady killer, who never killed any ladies, but was me friend. "Master Custard's me friend," Hector said. Wasn't that nice? And Little Lou who Bella ran through with the sword. Poor Little Lou, screaming blue murder. And Cousin Fred, ole Whistlin' Fred, who played the tin whistle real good, but had a terrible temper when he got mad.

"*Yaaaaah,*" yelled Custard, leaping up all of a sudden and bellowing far and wide. Though liking peace and quiet himself, being able when aroused to make more noise than a barnyard.

"Is that my friend Hector there?"

Up he leapt and up he ran, bellowing all around, bellowing, bellowing, *"Hector, Hector, are you there, here I am."*

Goodness, what a noise.

Into a wall of muscle and bone he crashed, into dank-smelling cloth he crashed.

It wasn't Hector at all.

Hector was sixteen and *this* fellow was older than Noah, and had bleary-lookin' eyes with whiskers all round.

"I've got the little perisher," the horrible fella screeched. "He's alive. He's kickin'. If he kicks one more time I'll punch him up the snout."

That's torn it, thought Custard. A real livin' spook, an' smellin' somethin' awful.

chapter twenty-two

MANY-HEADED MONSTER

THE SOFT WORLD of cliffs and crevasses of steam changed into something not foreseen.

Open up your eyes, young Custard, the bustard, the dreamer, the flute, and blink out your tears, and find a desert there, green as green.

> A desert green
> As a bean,
> Is it there,
> Is it there?
>
> Who never said
> In his head,
> Desert's red,
> Desert's red,
>
> Or overheard
> From a bird,
> Desert red
> Is the word,
>
> Or ever saw
> Furthermore
> Deserts red
> By the score?

> A desert green
> As a bean
> Must be green
> As a pear,
>
> To be there.

That soft world of mists and steam went swirling up to wallow and flare and then to be gone forevermore.

Clear sky grew as blue as the ages before, and underneath lay the moss and the rocks and the green of the land, and Custard was there, as were tent flies and wheelbarrows and men everywhere.

Any moment now a coach would crash in, striking sparks on stones, driver hailing, bringing news of Sydney Town. "Hey, have you heard?"

Well, Custard hoped it would. Then he'd run. And he'd run. And he'd leap to the driver up there. "Mr. Driver, take me home to my mum."

The bleary-eyed fella with the whiskers all round plucked him up like a stalk, took him up by the scruff, and set him down.

Lor, thought Custard.

I've been here before, thought Custard.

Look at it over there, that cliff, with the water pouring off!

We've been walking for a week and not going any place!

Got up on his feet, Ole Tommy did, and away he went. Day after day on through the wet, me sitting on that horse with a leg tied up, slish-slosh, water pouring down me neck. But there stand the rocks in the very same place. Dinosaurs all green from feeling so old I expect, and whales all green from sleepin' too long and forgetting to swim up to the top, and dragons all green from falling down plunk to the hard hard ground where St. Custard rides the horse.

Been here before. It's a fact.

So the bleary-eyed fella picked him up by the scruff and he felt his neck stretch.

"Aaarrrchchch," said Custard.

In crowded the people to stare, as if he had a tail like a devil's thumping on the floor, though it was his fist beating there, into his hip.

The terrible things that happen.

In they crowded, all those fellas, all with bleary-lookin' eyes and whiskers around. A real shockin' sight, to be sure.

"The Goose," they said.

Sighing they were, and panting, and rubbing at their bleary little eyes as if they were suffering from conjunctive-whatsit, and whistling through their whiskers, and spitting out juicy gobs a yard long or more.

Schlopp, when they hit the floor.

Disgustin', thought Custard.

"Gawd," they said.

"Strike me," they said.

"He's real," they said.

"The Goose," they said.

Don't see no goose, thought Custard, looking every-where. Don't see much round here except dirty-lookin' fellas all a-pushin' and a-shovin' and a-smellin' like a wet cow yard.

"Poo," said Custard.

Though not too loud in case they heard.

Grizzled and grimy and smeared they were, like the faces of old cards worn from grubby hands and grubby years. Skinny they were, and haggard and hollow and drawn. And the longer Custard looked, the more of them there were.

Making eleven to start with, he reckoned. And six more makes fifteen. And four makes twenty-two, or somethin' like it. Why don't the beggars stand still while I'm counting? I'll betcha there are forty. I'll betcha there are fifty.

The trooper wasn't there because no one had stripes on his pants.

Mum wasn't there because there weren't any ladies.

Seth wasn't there because no one was screaming at him to hoe the row or fetch the bucket.

Bella wasn't there because no one was hopping on sticks.

Hector wasn't there because no one had firestones round his neck from the whip that Custard had cracked, from the lash that Custard had whacked round Hector's neck. "Wahhh," Hector had screamed at the time.

Preacher Tom wasn't there, poor ole fella.

Just about everybody else was there, though, like the heads of a many-headed monster, all peerin' and blearin' and blinkin' and breathin' gusts of putridity into the air, with lots of spare legs and arms besides, for chasing kids up trees and over walls and for scrunching 'em with.

It'd be better if I made 'em disappear, thought Custard.

> Inkle dwinkle
> Ubba and tinkle,
> Twinkle winkle
> Grubba Magoo.

But there they stood and there they stood and there stood he. Never was much of a spell.

"Get an eyeful," they said. "It's him. He's real."

"Little squirt, isn't he?"

"Bag o' bones strung together with skin."

"Ain't he supposed to be thirteen?"

If they're talking about me, Custard grumbled to himself, I'm fourteen, depending on the day, and I ain't all that terrible. I can hoe the row as good as a man.

"What day is it?" he demanded aloud, annoyed.

"Eh?" said the monster with the heads.

"What day is it?" Custard demanded, "because if it's the thirteenth of March it's me birthday, and that makes me fourteen, and when I'm fourteen I'm grown up."

"February, innit?" said one head.

"Tuesday, I reckon," said another.

"He don't look old enough to have a birthday, unless half of him's down a hole!"

Blurts to you, thought Custard, feeling round with his foot for a stone to stand on, and going on with his counting until he got to sixty-four, while the heads went on muttering about the Goose and the Preacher and Gawd Save Us, and who'd believe the old coot'd snuff it and leave us holdin' the kid?

"They hang you for kidnapping kids."

"They hang you for killing preachers."

"If them fellas catch you and your name ain't Sir Dogsbody McSword they hang you because you're alive."

Goodness, thought Custard, do they really? All this time waiting for that trooper and that's what he'd do!

There was a wail going on somewhere. *"He's a lovely ole fella and he's dead."*

"Hector, Hector," Custard cried. "Where are you?"

chapter twenty-three

GOOSE FOR GOLD

CUSTARD COULDN'T SEE OUT because the monster was all around like a wall.

"Hector," he cried.

"You killed our dad," someone shrilled, screeching. "We'd all get rich, you said, even my poor old dad. We only had to wait, you said, until he dug the golden hole. You never said you'd shoot him dead."

It wasn't Hector though.

"He killed hisself," someone shouted back. "Chargin' out of the fog, scarin' me to death. I didn't pull no trigger. It jarred in me hand."

"You killed my dad."

A wailing arose, such as few had heard in the desert since the great stones had stirred, Custard joining in, because Preacher Tom being dead was like his father Adam being dead.

"Oh, it's troubles we've got," the many-headed creature cried, "and ain't it bad enough juss bein' alive! They'll hang us now. There's nothin' they like more than the nailing up of the heads of the poor."

That monster was waving its hands and turning its heads and bits were breaking from its sides. Away the bits went, looking for their wheelbarrows and their swags. Some started throwing punches and shouting *come back here, you lily-livered cur. Stickin' together and backin' each other up is the only hope of staying alive in this wicked world.*

One fellow shouted, "I can't stand yowling kids. If you don't stop yowling I'll punch you so far you'll meet yourself coming back."

Looming over Custard he was, with a fist big enough to lift him off the ground for a couple of years.

So Custard stopped his yowling and said to himself, "Being alive is bad enough without getting scrunched."

What was left of the many-headed monster, those bits not heading for the hills, started shuffling round him again. And the wailing in the desert faded like a wave running back from the shore. And the sun turned into a fiery ball.

"Bah," said Custard.

"Everything was real good," the monster said.

"Following him we was, taking real good care not to break any laws. Not a law in the land could've nailed us."

"Keepin' an eye on the kid in a law-abidin' legal manner we was, makin' sure he was safe and sound. Upholding the Queen's justice, Gord bless her, until the beautiful yellow stuff was flowing and time was right and proper for cashing him in on the reward."

"Winning from both ends," the monster said, "like the rich folks."

"But lose we do."

"Like the likes of us always do," the monster said.

"And not a sign of gold, so what in Hell was the Preacher cheering about?"

Bah, thought Custard. Always some fella expectin' me to make him rich, and I ain't even got a pair of socks.

"Bah," he yelled, "you're all mad. I never found no gold in my whole life. I wanna go home."

"Pipe down, kid," the monster said.

"Yeh, kid, we've got enough troubles, startin' from way back before you was born."

"There ain't no gold," Custard yelled.

"Not yet there ain't," the monster said.

"Bah," yelled Custard.

Sitting on that slish-sloshing horse, he'd been, with rain pouring in his ears and pouring down his neck, pouring down his pants and filling up his boots, and not any dinner in a week!

He banged on the ground with two angry fists.

"Where's this here goose? I'm havin' her egg. I'm having it hard-boiled. I'm having it right now. You'd better get it quick."

"Gawd," the monster said, "listen to the kid."

"I'm sick of bein' the goose," yelled Custard.

"That's right, kid," the monster said, "you're the Goose."

Custard's mouth snapped shut.

"You're the Goose," they said, "the gorgeous Goose."

I'm the goose, thought Custard, and not a feather in me chest?

"You'll have to lay the egg yourself," the monster said.

"I'm a rooster. I can't lay eggs."

"It depends," said the monster.

"It don't," said Custard. "I never laid one yet."

"Golden Gooses do," they said. "Golden Gooses lay gorgeous golden eggs."

Lor, thought Custard.

No goose for roasting.

No goose for eggs.

Just goose for gold.

And I'm it!

"Waaaaah," came a wailing from the desert, a wailing starting up again like the wave running back. "My farver don't breave no more. My farver ain't never going to come home no more and tell us stories. I ain't got nuffin' now, but me bruvvers and me cousin Fred, and who'd want them?"

That was Hector.

You always knew when it was Hector.

"You got me, Hector," cried Custard.

"He was a nice ole fella," wailed Hector, "and never did no one harm. Riding round the country on his pony. Giving away his tucker. Giving away his pennies. Nuffin' left for us at home but stories."

"I'm still here, Hector," cried Custard.

"Now he's gone," wailed Hector, "just because you had to have a gun wiv a bullet in it. Now there ain't even a story."

"There's me," cried Custard.

"Waaaaah," wailed Hector.

"I haven't got no dad neither, Hector, to bake me a loaf or tell me a story."

"Are you hungry, kid?" the monster said to Custard.

"I'm starvin'," said Custard. "I want a hard-boiled egg with some nice hot bread and I don't want it burnt with ashes in it, either."

"I don't boil eggs so good," said one of the heads of the monster, "but I'm good with a story. There were these three bears, see. One built his house out of bricks and one built his house out of sticks and the third had bacon for supper with Worcestershire sauce on it. His grandad cooked the bacon because his auntie had gone to market in a wheelbarrow."

Lor, thought Custard.

"And there was this 'ere fairy-godmother," said another head, "what grew pumpkins and turned 'em into porridge. And these hundreds of kids were runnin' round chewin' the legs off the tables because they couldn't stand no more porridge. All the time buying new tables she was. Kept her in the poorhouse, poor ole fairy godmother. Every time she worked another spell it turned into another plate of porridge. You never saw so many tables with their legs bitten off."

Lor, thought Custard.

"I'm coming, Hector," he hollered, and away he rushed, bursting out through the side of the monster.

"Here I am, Hector," yelled Custard. "This is your friend Custard calling. Don't you go away. Answer me, Hector, or the monster'll get me."

chapter twenty-four

LIFE IS BUT
A GUESSING GAME

WHERE WAS HECTOR? Where was he?

Custard drew a mighty breath. "Hector, Hector, are you there?"

"Is that my friend?" Hector called.

"Yeh, oh yeh," Custard hollered.

"Here I am," Hector called.

"Where, oh where?" Custard hollered.

"Where he killed our farver."

Life is but a guessin' game, thought Custard.

One old fellow was passing there, scratched and bloodied, jacket torn, as if going home from war. Using a musket to prop himself up, limping and swaying and weaving and lamenting:

"Blinded I am, never again to see the livelong day. Like in the wicked times of yore, of red-hot irons used for the maiming of the helpless and the poor.

"Ah, me eyes is scratched away, and it's a horrible fate for a helpless soul so far from hearth and home.

"No one to lead him by the hand.

"No one to say, *no no,* not there, you'll walk into a black man's spear and be impaled as upon a skewer rotating o'er the flame.

"Or, *no no,* not there, you'll fall down a hole and on your head you'll land, to penetrate the sand, and like a dying tree stark an' awful stand.

"And I didn't pull the trigger, I swear.

"As they come chargin' through, rooted to the ground I were.

"Victim of the fates. The devil's helpless pawn.

"And oh my gawd, what's that I see a-standing there?

"The Goose, the fiend it is, with claws."

And off he ran another way, crying as he went:

"Just a helpless ole man I am. I'll break his blasted jaw.

"I'll kill, I'll kill, I will, I will, I'll feed him to the crows.

"But if eyes is eyes and none I've got as I surmise, what did I see him with?

"Oh my gawd, me eyes is there and workin' still.

"Oh, I luvs you. Oh, I luvs you, one and all."

And off he rushed from man to man kissing everyone he saw.

"Go away," they shrieked. "You horrible hairy old gnome."

"Hector, Hector," Custard hollered, "you don't tell me where to go, and me I'm on me own."

Coming through the scrub he came, Hector calling as he came, "Master Custard, here I am. Night and day following you and my old man. Always near. Here I am."

Running through the scrub he came, Custard's only friend, and only for a day.

"Hector, Hector," Custard cried, "and you're really really real."

Hector, running through the scrub, neck ringed round by firestones to remind him of the day.

Custard, long ago, long ago, and the whip he cracked, and up Hector leapt and back he fell, his neck ringed round with firestones.

"Hector, Hector," Custard cried, "my very friend has come."

"My farver's dead," Hector sobbed.

"I know."

"A terrible ole farver he was," Hector sobbed, "always going away and leaving us at home."

"Poor thing," said Custard, stroking Hector's head.

My friend, thought Custard. My very friend. His nose is like Preacher Tom's but not as big.

The Lady Killer, Hector was, but now looked thin and drawn and sad. He'd not be killing ladies again, for a little while, though the ladies that he killed were never really dead and didn't really mind.

"My friend," Custard said, and went away with him through the scrub, bits of the monster trailing on behind, looking glum.

"All this suffering," the monster said. "All these miles and miles and miles. All for nothing?"

Poor old monster.

chapter twenty-five

THE PILGRIM'S CROWN

JAMIE THE CAPTAIN, the general, sat with his legs crossed like an Indian gentleman reflecting upon serious matters. In the cradle of his lap Preacher Tom lay sleeping.

Preacher Tom slept in the lap of his first-born son, never again to leap up shouting, never again to rant or thunder, never again to come creeping through the hut door long after the candle sputtered, creeping round the floor, creeping from son to son, kissing each one, whispering tender as a mother, "Good night, my son. God take care of thee until the glorious morning. God refresh thee in thy slumber and profit thee when thou wakest, me precious darlin' boy."

"No one wanted him to be perfect," sniffed Jamie.

Cousin Fred, ole Whistlin' Fred, said, "Now I'm a orphan. Such a lovely ole uncle and me not havin' another, one like him bein' enough for any fella."

Little Lou, usually plump like a kitten because he got the butter, but emaciated from his recent sufferings, was wailing something dreadful, Little Lou being given to noise-making about most subjects painful. "Stop y' blubbin', Lou," they'd have said, if they'd not been blubbing also.

"My dad's dead," wailed Lou, "all because of us, my dad's dead. All because of you, ole Jamie, my dad's dead. All because of you, ole Custard, my dad's dead. Now I ain't got no dad to pat me on the head."

Kenrick van der Mellow Mere, far from the nearest harbour, a-sailin' o'er the sea, rose up in his hammock in the creaking darkness, crying out loud to all that listened, mainly wood-worm and deathwatch beetle, the ships of the Indian Pacific Line being a bit run down. "Something's happened to my dad, I fear, 'cos he just come to me real near. Ken, me darlin' boy, he said, farewell to thee until some other year."

So Cousin Fred, and Hector the Lady Killer, and Little Lou, and Custard the bustard, and Jamie the general, took turns at digging the hole through the mud and the gravel and the rocks, and baling out the water, because water was running pretty close to the surface. Then they laid him out and lowered him, the Preacher fella with the noblest nose and the finest turn of phrase sleeping west of the Blue Mountains, and filled him in.

"Oh lor," cried Jamie, "it's me gorgeous dad."

"It's me dad," wailed Little Lou.

Hector's jaw trembled in a manly manner and Cousin Fred played a tune on his whistle.

> Up them stairs the weary plod,
> Leaning on the pilgrim rod,
> On him falls the heartless sod,
> Our Ole Tommy's gone to God.

Sing Golden Goose,
Sing Golden Goose,
Sing Golden Goose, my hearty.

They made a cross ready, Custard making it, Custard being the expert with sticks, no one disputing it.

Standing there was Custard, waiting with his sticks, waiting to tap them in with the little hammer that Prospector Tom used for breaking up rock.

Thinking deep and gloomy, was Custard, holding onto the cross, a real impatient little cross it was, pulling and tugging and feeling peculiar. All that water lying about, and all the bones no doubt, while Fred went on playing his tune, putting in some trills. Then the cross broke free from Custard and arrowed into the head of the heap.

"Watcha throw it for?" yowled Jamie.

"I didn't throw it," yowled Custard.

"You did," yowled Jamie.

"I didn't. It's all the water lying about and all those bones down underneath."

"What bones?" yowled Jamie.

"His bones," yowled Custard.

So they all blubbed a bit more.

Hector put the tall black hat in front of the cross and held it in place with a pretty little rock washed clean in a puddle. Handsome that hat looked, too, sitting there, but Lou wailed that he couldn't stand the sight of it no more and ran off weeping, and Jamie and Fred and Hector were sniffing hard on their noble Roman noses and wiping them

on their sleeves, and Custard went on looking at the pretty
little rock.

My goodness, thought Custard.

There they were, way out in the desert, if desert it could
be called, just the five of them, Custard being fifth-in-com-
mand, seein' ole Kenrick was a sailor for the time being,
and nothing being left of Preacher Tom except the shape
of him, and the tent flies being gone, and the wheelbarrows
being gone, and all the bits of the many-headed monster
being gone, and nothing being left in the green desert but
the everlasting dripping of the water and Little Horse
chewing on the vegetation, burping from a surfeit of greens
and wattle blossom.

My goodness goodness, thought Custard. It is, you
know; a lump as big as a tea-cup sitting on his hat!

Like Ole Tommy said. Saw it clear. The Age of Gold
beginning right here.

"Gug," croaked Custard.

Custard, the bustard, the singer, the mute.

The mourners went on weeping their sorrows and saying their prayers, asking God to take real good care of the
old bloke, because he was so gorgeous, and to give him a
nice new Bible with pages 221 to 224 not torn out by
kids, meaning Hector, twelve years ago or thereabouts,
when he was four and horrible.

"Gug," croaked Custard, the mourners going on with
their supplicating, asking God to arrange for the ole fella's
potatoes to be baked nice and crisp, and for a nice high
pillow for his bed, and for a real nice lady to be waitin'

there, who wouldn't want to be arguing if he came home late from his preaching.

"Gold," croaked Custard, getting louder by a bit.

"Old?" said Jamie.

"Gold," croaked Custard, inhaling with a racking cough.

"Cold?" said Jamie.

"Gold," shrieked Custard, *"on his hat."*

chapter twenty-six

MY GOODNESS

"Gwooo," said Jamie.

Nobody else said anything for a while.

They were looking quite furtive, quite guilty, as if turning directly to each other was not allowed.

Then they started changing colour. Fred went white. Jamie turned green.

"Gwooo," said Jamie, having another try, and backed off as if he needed more room.

"Oh my gawd," wheezed Hector, as if all the air for breathing had blown away.

"Gowwwllld," said Jamie, "onnnn hhisss hhaaattt." Though it didn't sound like that. Sounded more like Jamie choking to death.

Fred started stuttering, his teeth breaking into a chatter. "I'm g-g-g-gunna be sick."

"The biggest hunk of gold in the world," wheezed Hector, though no one understood a word he said.

Making the most extraordinary noises they were, the whole lot of them.

"Big enough to buy a carriage and pair with," choked Jamie.

"Big enough to bub-bub-buy a piana with," stuttered Fred.

"Big enough to buy a walkin' cane and a velvet coat," wheezed Hector, "wif red silk linings."

"It'll be buying' nothin'," said Little Lou, "because it's me dad's."

"Wh-wh-what's that you say?" stuttered Fred.

"It's me dad's," said Lou. "Come out of his grave. It's on his hat."

"Big enough to bub-bub-buy a pup-pup-piana with," said Fred, "like I wuw-wanted from the ssstart."

"It's on his hat," said Jamie, "like Lou says."

"Nun-nun-not in his hat though," said Fred, "not like he owned it. Like it fuf-fuf-fell on him."

"I could do with a gut-bucket meself," said Custard.

"It'll be buying a tombstone," said Lou.

"You could buy a hundred tombstones wiv it," said Hector.

"Two hundred," said Fred.

"Lor," said Jamie. "Worth as much as that?"

"It'll buy a real nice tombstone," said Lou.

"I thought I was the captain of the Buttons," said Jamie.

"The bub-bub-baby-faced squ-squirt," said Whistling Fred, his teeth chattering something awful, "fuf-fuf-fifth-in-command, that's all he is."

"Fourth," said Lou, "now that Ken's not here."

"Ffffourth then," said Fred.

"A tombstone," said Lou, "and a nice little chapel with a bell tower on top, seein' you say there's so much of it.

God's House, me dad used to say he'd call it. We'll call it St. Tom's."

"Lor," said Jamie, shocked.

"I fink the ole fella would like that," said Hector.

"St. Tom's," said Jamie, with half a shriek.

"A very nice name I fink, said Hector.

"Lor," said Jamie, "I don't think we can call him a saint. He was a bit of a lad with the ladies."

"What's wrong wiv being nice to the ladies?" said Hector. "It says in the Bible you've got to love everybody."

"It don't mean it the way you do," said Jamie.

"Where's it say that then?" said Hector.

"P'raps it was on those pages you pulled out when you were a little kid."

"What I sssays," said Fred, "is that this here Ggggoose should cut hisself another sssstick and fffind another bit. That'll settle it."

"I was about to say the same meself," said Jamie.

"Well you didn't," said Fred. "I said it."

"I fink it's a very good idea," said Hector. "Cut yourself a stick, Master Custard."

"What for?" said Custard.

"You know what for," said Hector.

"Come on," urged Jamie, the captain, the general, "like as if you was goin' to do it for me dad."

"I can't find gold," said Custard. "I don't know what gold looks like."

"You do," yowled Jamie, " 'cos there it is on his hat."

"I never found no gold in my whole life," wailed Custard,

"or I'd have found it for my mum."

"You did too," yowled Jamie, "there's that great box she's got full of it."

"I keep on sayin' it," yelled Custard. *"I never found no gold in my whole life."*

"My poor ole dad," cried Lou, "lyin' there, and all this shoutin' and screamin' goin' on. I think it's right disgusting."

Strike me purple, thought Custard, and whipped out his knife, all of them jumping back, even Hector his friend.

"Grrrrrr," said Custard, breathing in snorts, his hair standing on end, his teeth showing.

He slashed a stick from the nearest bush and stripped the leaves from it and threw them at his feet and jumped on them.

"Grrrrrr," said Custard.

"My gawd," said Hector.

"If I had a gun I'd shoot you," cried Custard. "If I had a lion he'd eat you. I'm going home in a minute and who tries to stop me gets turned into a grub. Never found no gold in my whole life I haven't."

He laid the forked stick on his hands and barely had a grip on it before it pulled through his shoulders. Like a break in the wall of a dam it was. Away he stumbled behind it and down it speared into a puddle.

"There," he shrieked. "See!"

Then he went rigid from the knees up.

Then he started thinking back.

"Lor," said Custard.

Water underground never felt like that. And it wasn't

the ole fella's bones, because they were away over there. Iron never felt like it neither.

"Oh grrrrrr," he yelled at the sky, "I hate you. Another week of rain comin'. I'll die. I'll drown. I can't stand no more of it. I'm sick to death of getting wet."

"What's that stick doing there?" demanded Jamie.

"Stickin' in the ground," wailed Custard, "like when the storm started. Just the same."

"What storm?" said Jamie, looking everywhere about.

"Give it a minute," wailed Custard. "It'll be back."

"I don't see no storm," said Whistlin' Fred. "Trying to put us off, that's your game."

He plucked out the stick and drove in the spade.

Big fellow was Fred, going on eighteen, good at splitting slabs with an axe. Drove the spade down and almost dislocated his neck.

"Yow," yelped Fred, grabbing for his wrists and hugging at his arms and rubbing at his neck. "What was that?"

"What was what?" said Jamie, having a fit of the insecures, because it was bound to be his fault.

"Wasn't no puddle," said Hector.

"Stun me," moaned Fred, rocking on his feet. "Me neck."

"Stand back then," said Jamie, drawing himself up. "I'm the captain."

"Jamie's the captain," said Hector.

Fred wasn't arguing just then.

Jamie worked the spade round and levered it up.

"It's a rock," he said.

Over there, Custard noted, the sun was at about eight o'clock, not a sign of cloud, not a sign of storm, just that ole sun shining long and low, casting its morning shadows, lighting up the puddles, sparkling in the leaves, gleaming on Jamie's rock.

"Me neck," moaned Fred.

Everyone except Fred looked at the rock.

"Arr," said Jamie.

"Arr," said Lou.

"What's that you're lookin' at?" said Fred.

"Arr," said Hector.

"Is that my bit of rock?" said Fred.

"It's our bit of rock," said Jamie.

"Give it a wash," said Fred.

Jamie splashed water from the puddle and gave it a rub.

"Arr," said Jamie.

A real pretty rock it was, looking molten, like a piece of slag from a furnace, about the size of a brick.

"My goodness," said Custard.

"Gwoo," said Jamie.

"Yoweeeeeeee," shrieked ole Whistlin' Fred, leaping up and running round and turning somersaults on his stiff neck, *we done it, we done it, we done it, we done it, we done it."*

"I fink," yelled Hector in Fred's direction, "that you'd better be quiet, or all them fellas will be coming back down from the hills and we won't have done it at all."

"Yeh," yelled Jamie. *"Shut up, Fred."*

Fred stopped turning somersaults and went back to

rubbing his neck, which felt worse. "All right, but there's no need to be rude. *We done it, don't you know!*"

"Those fellas have got guns," said Lou, "and we've got nothin'."

"We've got the Goose," said Fred, grinning through his teeth.

"You ain't got the Goose," said Custard. "I've got meself from now on. No one else is gettin' me either, or I'll go home."

"Yeh," said Jamie, "so shut up, Fred."

"Yeh, Fred," said Hector, "be nice to my friend, Master Custard."

"Yeh," said Lou.

"Sink me," said Fred, "what you all pickin' on me for? This is time for celebratin'. We're rich! *We're rich as kings.*"

"Shut up, Fred," said Jamie, "or we'll all be dead as ducks. There's real bad men in that lot. So how are we goin' to divide up the gold? What have we got to cut it with?"

"Cut it?" squealed Fred.

"Shut up, Fred," said Jamie. "Why don't you keep your mouth shut!"

"Cut the gold?" said Hector.

"You shut up, too, Hector," said Jamie.

"You don't cut gold," said Hector. "You melt it."

"You don't melt it," yowled Fred. "You sell it."

"I wish you could eat it," said Custard.

"We could always find some more," said Lou, "and have a piece each."

"*A piece each?*" screeched Hector.

"Why not?" said Lou.

"You don't find gold lyin' all over the place, you silly thing."

"We found two bits already, haven't we?"

"We have, you know," said Jamie. "We've found two bits already."

Fred nodded. "We've found two bits already."

Hector thought about it. "Two bits already."

"One for me dad," said Lou, "so that leaves only one we found. We got to get three more."

"Four," said Hector.

"What do you want four for?" asked Lou.

"One for Master Custard," said Hector.

"He don't want one," said Lou. "He can find it any time he wants it."

"Can I?" said Custard.

"Of course you can."

"You mean I can find gold any time I want it?" said Custard.

"Like you had it in a box somewhere and only had to take it out."

"Wow," said Custard.

"If it's all that easy," said Fred, "why don't we find two bits each?"

"Shut up, Fred," said Jamie. "Two bits each?"

"Don't see why not," said Fred.

"Two bits each," whistled Hector. "As big as this one here?"

"Maybe bigger."

"There ain't that much gold in the world."

"There will be soon," said Lou, "I reckon."

Very sharp was Little Lou. They hadn't realized he was growing up to be such a sharp fella.

So they stood there for a while getting used to the idea, kind of listening to their hearts going thud, kind of awed by it all. Not just little bits of gold like pimples or peas, but lumps of gold like rocks for doorstops.

Very quiet it was standing there.

So quiet, they could hear that greedy little horse rumbling in his tum. They could also hear something that sounded like a cattle stampede.

"What's that?" said Lou.

"My gawd," wailed Hector.

Jamie shrieked at Fred, "You and your big mouth, screeching like some crazy owl! All those fellas comin' now! Look at 'em runnin' now!"

It must be what they mean by the gold rush, thought Custard.

chapter twenty-seven

THE GLADIATORS

THEY CAME DOWN from the hills, leaping and legging along the gullies, across the creeks, through the scrub, waving shovels and guns, as if obstacles were not there, as if trees stood only to be knocked aside, as if anything less than the height of a man was destined for death by man's hand.

Two, as if running a gladiatorial race, came rushing to the brink of the bluff. Suddenly they were there, up there, running straight on over the edge of the bluff, running to level ground far below, running through the air, tumbling, until the air was gone. Then they made not another move nor another sound.

It was like an explosion in the eyes.

Something awful was happening.

It was violent and mad and cold.

Custard knew these things as if someone had spelt them out and explained.

"Lor," Jamie said in a small boy's voice, though Jamie was in most things a man. He reached out for Fred's arm, to hold, to feel near, to say to Fred without saying it, Forget that I shouted at you. I'm scared.

"Yeh," said Fred.

Guns were shooting off in the gullies, though shooting back there was a waste of time.

Men were leaving their wheelbarrows back there. Wheelbarrows belonged to an age that had gone.

Men were turning to each other, as if to enemies never before seen. Everywhere they looked they saw gold for others, but none in their own hands. Armies marched through their brains. They saw kings and queens taking the gold away in wagon trains.

They grabbed shovels and hatchets and guns.

They left their wheelbarrows upended, their swags torn apart. They left their possessions of the world strewn on the ground, and began to run furiously as if the last coach to Glory were coming over the mountains of the Great Divide.

For some the coach had gone.

There was a terrible change. No man wished it or willed it, but it came.

Each face came separately, as if flecked by madness, as if close up, even though each was a distance away.

Behind them into the hills rolled the sound.

"The Goose. The gold."

They came like a mindless rabble, mad from deprivation, charging in to carve up the remains, as if to loot and kill and burn, as if women and children were to be destroyed first without a qualm.

Lucky for the women they were not there.

Not a place on the plain was left for boys.

Everything was transparent there. The landscape was flattened or erased.

There was nowhere to hide.

In the shock, in the panic, their limbs became as stone, because these men coming like a plague were not like the men who yarned around fires singing songs about the Golden Goose while Whistlin' Fred played the tune.

Their faces had changed.

This was different from bandit kingdoms beside the sea; different from carrying off kids thirteen years old who didn't really mind; different from Jamie Button, the captain, the general, running stupid wild, no matter how fierce he sounded or how lawless were his plans.

Men running stupid wild were giants in the land, and ran over kids as if they were ants or snails or paths.

Perhaps the dinosaurs on the plain, and the whale, giants though they were in former times, had been caught by the same panic when greater giants made the gold.

There they'd stand, Jamie and Fred and Hector and Custard and Lou, like the dragons, turned to stone.

Little Horse bolted across the plain, some men trying to bring him down. Horses were made of gold of another kind, but Little Horse fled away.

Someone with a gun took the lump of gold like a doorstop from Jamie or Fred or Hector.

The man with the gun had a terrible, feverish wildness in him and was spitting all around, "Out of my way. I'll blow your brains out. I'll spatter 'em."

Custard saw the man running, saw someone catch him with a jagged rock fiercely thrown. Then the one who threw the stone took up the gun and the lump of gold and ran.

Someone else threw a stone.

The man blundered into the mob and screamed.

Preacher Tom's tall black hat was gone, and the piece of gold for his tombstone was gone, and boots drove through his grave and scattered the pots and pans.

Jamie shrieked and tried to stand up tall.

Fred started yelling, "What are you doing to us all?"

Hector screamed words that Custard had never heard before, and went out fighting, as if hitting might fix it, but a gun went off.

There was a flash from Hector's eyes that signalled the most dire disappointment in the world for a boy.

"Hector," said Custard vaguely, as on a battlefield, and sat beside his friend and held a limp warm hand.

Someone said, "Here's your stick, kid. Get real busy with it. There ain't much time."

Preacher Tom's cross was thrust into his hands.

They're going to kill us all, thought Custard.

"I don't know where the gold is," he said to the man. "They took it away."

Jamie was lying on the ground and Fred was heaped against a tree and Lou was sprawled across the grave and Hector was already far away.

I'm not dreaming it, thought Custard.

Someone said, "There's a price on the kids. They'd have got hung, anyway."

"Get busy, kid," people kept on saying, planting Custard like a cabbage, as if to say, *grow*.

He wilted instead.

Like leaves in a whirlwind, men hammered pegs into the ground. All around the grave they hammered pegs into the ground. In rows, in blocks, like wedges of crazy paving, as close as they could crowd to the grave.

All these people rushing about with hatchets cutting pegs; they were mad.

Custard couldn't quite see what he saw, yet knew it was happening there.

They pointed him this way. They pointed him another way. He held the cross and it didn't pull or twitch or swerve. They propped him up when his legs were too weak to stand.

The world was full of desperate people threatening and pushing at each other, and threatening and pushing at Custard, full of angry swearing, angry shouting, and desperate cries.

Some stood chest to chest, disputing ground, trading blows with anything at hand. Two, like territorial cats, fought with knives and no one cared. One ran off in despair, as if about to cry. Custard saw his eyes, saw his bleeding hands. The man hammered in his pegs farther out.

They were shouting at Custard.

"He's an idiot."

Someone struck him with the flat of a shovel, though it caused no pain that he felt for a while.

He wandered off as if following secret lines drawn on the ground.

The vagueness in his head was like the mist of the

bright golden morning. Sometimes he saw through. Other times it was a cloud.

Farther out and farther out men hammered at pegs, jealous of every inch they could hold or gain. Some built fences, furiously hammering sticks into the ground. Axes rang. Trees fell.

Farther out and farther out yet another pair of hands would plant Custard like a cabbage and say, "Come on, Goose. Show us where."

Then people would start jostling again.

"He's stupid."

"He's a fraud."

Men were digging into mud, into slush, baling out with hats and hands and billycans. Everywhere men were yellow with sprays of water and sprays of mud. Everywhere men were mad.

Custard sat on a rock in the shade and with the long shaft of Preacher Tom's cross drew circles in the mud, or lines, or curves, drawing them one over the other until it was like a map charting the courses of planets and stars. Water bled in from the mud and filled the lanes. Water came down from the cliff behind and flowed around. Not far away two men lay dead in the mud from running through the air like gladiators.

"Gold!"

Others still came crashing in through the scrub, labouring in the mud, fatigued to sickness from running so hard, so far; some collapsing, some vomiting, others continuing to run in different directions, as if distracted or afraid.

Some came over to Custard, to peer at him, then quickly went away.

"He's snapped in the brain, but still worth two hundred quid, you know. Do you reckon he'd live till we got him home?"

"I wouldn't touch him with a forty-foot pole.'

Others said, "Did you see them blokes killed? Gold or no, I'm on me way. Gawd, but how can a man leave? You could be rich for life in a day."

"Gold!"

More men came down through the hills, came exhausted, came running, or came wild.

None went away.

More dug holes and more dug holes and everywhere they ran around with pegs and hatchets and picks and shovels.

"How much are you allowed? How much ground?"

"Gold!"

Custard sat on his rock, and no one came close, except to peer, then to go away, for the bodies were there, only paces away, and no one knew who'd put them there and no one was ready for the blame. And the kid was in a stupor, something wrong with his brain. Being near him was bad.

"Gold!"

Gold was over there, over where the shouting was, where the fights were, where the yells rose above the crowd.

In the shadows of his mind, Custard made a song as he sat on his rock.

> O Father God, from whom it comes
> As Preacher Tom has told,
> Why have you made this awful stuff,
> This awful, awful gold?
>
> My friend is dead and gone away,
> I'd rather have him near,
> Than all the gold and all the gold
> And all the gold that's here.

That's a real terrible song, thought Custard, and began to cry.

After he was able to open his eyes the sun had moved onto his neck, and was hot and high, and everything stank of dank mud, and two boots with holes in them like open mouths planted themselves at his side.

They belonged to Lou.

It's startin', thought Custard. Here come the spooks.

So he poked at the spook to make it go away, but Lou was solid. Real solid mud was Lou, which was nice.

Custard shuffled across his rock until there was room for two.

"There's no one left but us," said Lou, sitting there, sitting down good and solid. Sitting there alive. Most of him was mud, but you could see something like blood in his hair and two black eyes.

Custard was glad Lou was there.

"Everyone's got gold," said Lou. "What have we got?"

Custard thought about that.

Tears welled up in Lou and such a cry came from him

that Custard at once felt older and stronger, and hugged him, even though he felt shy.

"Poor Lou," he said.

"I haven't got anywhere now," cried Lou, "not anywhere anywhere. And I haven't got me lovely mum or me lovely dad or me lovely brothers. I haven't even got Fred."

"You've got me," said Custard, remembering he'd said it before, though it was to Hector then.

"Yeh," said Lou, going quiet.

"I'll take care of you," said Custard.

"You're younger than I am," said Lou.

"You can take care of me too," said Custard.

"I can make Johnny cakes," said Lou.

"I can eat 'em," said Custard.

They sat on the rock while the mob shouted and yelled and went on ringing their axes and chopping down their trees, went on hammering at pegs and pickets and settling disputes with fists and gun butts and awful screaming threats.

"Gold," they were shouting.

"Oh my gawd, gold," they were shouting.

"Gawd luv us, gold," they were shouting.

Custard and Lou sat on the rock for a long time because the world was mad.

Two strange-looking objects made of mud stumbled out from the mob, out over the pegs, out round the pickets, as if not knowing the way, as if very drunk as well. Reeling and falling and picking themselves up and groping on as if pushing through fog.

They were like a couple of new spooks who'd been people until lately, and hadn't become properly invisible, and were caught between night and day.

Custard glanced with suspicion at the two fellows who'd run over the cliff.

On came the two heaps of mud, if mud it were of which they were made, away from the mob, away from over there, reeling and staggering, crying one plaintive word:

"Lou!"

Lou went running to them, went leaping to them, went screaming to them, "Here I am, Jamie, Jamie! Here I am, Fred!"

"Poor Lou," said Custard, and waited for Lou to run through them, because Jamie and Fred were not there.

But Lou didn't run through them.

"Lor," said Custard. "They're still here. What about my friend Hector then?"

His heart leapt up and his spirit leapt up.

"Hector, Hector," Custard called.

Away he ran to where they were.

"Hector, Hector, are you there?

"Where's my friend Hector?" demanded Custard of Jamie or Fred, not knowing which was which, there being so much mud everywhere.

He wasn't sure they heard.

"Where's Hector?"

Perhaps they didn't know Custard was there.

Custard kicked his left ankle with his right toe and it

hurt like mad. "That's me," he said. "I'm real. Can't you see me?"

He went on down and in among the mad men, in among the pegs and pickets and heaps and holes. It was strange in there, nothing like before.

"Hector, Hector, where are you?"

He had to walk round holes and wade through oozes. He had to dodge showers of mud that were flying everywhere. He had to watch out for swinging picks and falling trees.

"Hector, Hector, answer me."

On went Custard through the maze.

Someone said as Custard passed with the cross in his hand, "The Goose has come."

Another heard, and said, "The Goose is here."

More looked around.

One, splitting pickets, drove his axe into the ground and left it there to quiver like a nerve.

Someone said, "They reckoned he'd run for his life."

Custard walked on through, picking his way. It was the ooze out of which the worlds were made. The strange labouring creatures that paused as he passed were the demons that puddled the mud and made the stones and afterwards sank back into the ooze again.

"The Goose. There he goes."

There was a stink in the ooze like sour old wells, and the demons knelt in it and waded in it and wallowed in it and breathed in it with awful sounds.

"The Golden Goose."

Custard went on through, but couldn't find Hector or Preacher Tom.

"Hector," cried Custard. "Where are you?"

Some put tools aside. Some sheathed knives. Some wondered why.

Some stood in the mud, sinking, legs braced or astride, chests heaving, breath grating, watching the boy go by.

"It's the Goose, they say."

"Hector, Hector," Custard cried very loud.

The fever broke with something like a sigh. The sigh became a silence that moved on the plain like a wave.

Custard couldn't find Hector anywhere. Perhaps Hector belonged to another place or another age.

Up and down, Custard wandered in the ooze.

He couldn't find Preacher Tom's grave.

"Here's the cross I made. It should be on the grave."

There was a silence on the plain, and men coming through the gullies, running and panting and pausing and running again, were arrested by the wave, and stopped, as if destination and purpose had suddenly disappeared.

"You've taken Preacher Tom and hidden him away. And where's my friend Hector gone, and the gold we found to build the church with the tall bell tower that we're going to call St. Tom's?"

There was silence on the plain, and in it his voice was clear, and each demon sinking in the ooze avoided other eyes, for who could tell where the dead might lie, or who would say if he knew?

The Goose was in the midst of them, accusing them.

They wished he'd go away.

chapter twenty-eight

FEATHERS IN OUR HATS, SIR

THEY BEGAN TO MURMUR among themselves on the plain. A few, like ostriches, started turning other ways, only to see eyes watching, warily. Some were terrified in their bones, and were terrified of the panic in themselves, for others might see the panic, and ask why.

No man had the courage to take up the swing of his pick or his axe again, to be the first to break the current of the wave, to be the first to say, *let's get back to grabbing our gold*.

No man had the nerve to accuse his neighbour, for by accusing his neighbour he would accuse himself.

There stood the boy they had followed through the days.

> Sing the Goose who did it, lads,
> Who found the El Dorado,
> Rich you'll be, as rich as me,
> With feathers in our hats, sir.
>
> Sing Golden Goose,
> Sing Golden Goose,
> Sing Golden Goose, my hearty.

Someone said, "We're rich, you know. It's true, you know."

Another said, "He found it."

Someone said, "Who took his gold?"

Another said, "We've got to stick together or they'll hang us."

"Give the kid his gold."

The murmuring began to move with a current of its own.

"Give the kid his gold."

"Who's got the kid's gold?"

The murmuring swelled and swayed, as if afraid, as if fearing every weapon that could kill a man or his neighbour, as if every man dreaded the savagery that might burst again like a storm.

"Who's got the kid's gold?"

"What mongrel took his gold?"

Custard stood in the midst of it and felt the winds.

Preacher Tom's grave wasn't anywhere around, no matter how hard he peered, or where. Hector wasn't there either.

Out on the plain the view had changed.

A horseman had come.

That was strange.

A horseman, looking like a picture of a horseman surveying a distant scene, was clearly there.

It could have been a spook though. Spooks were everywhere that day.

"Someone's got the kid's gold."

"It ain't me."

"Ain't me, neither. I never got a sniff of it."

They were shifting their hands on the axe handles, on the pick handles, on the shovels. They were changing grips to deliver quicker blows. Their breathing was an awful sound in the air. They were dragging their feet up from the ooze.

"We've all got his gold, I say!"

"You're crazy. I wasn't here till after."

"I wasn't either."

"Not just you, mate. The most of us. All that stuff happened before we got here."

They were terrified, even though they were mad. Every man wanted to be out of it, but every man went on with it, just the same.

Someone yelled, "The Goose found it, didn't he, or there wouldn't have been any gold for anyone?"

"He's a fraud. It's got nothin' to do with the Goose. He's an idiot."

"If anyone found it, it was the Preacher, and he's as dead as a tent-peg."

The horseman was coming nearer, which Custard thought was interesting.

It wasn't Little Horse coming back again either.

The rider rode steady and high, sitting up as straight as a soldier, and looking less like a spook at every stride.

In a minute one of these mad fellas would see him there.

"Yes, yes, the Preacher was here. Who said he wasn't? But this kid found it, and this kid's the Goose. Who is it we've been followin' for half a year?"

"We'll have a curse on us if we rob him."

"Yeh, a share for the Goose!"

The call became a sudden shout, became another wave, became a rhythm, became a great shout of deliverance.

"A share for the Goose."

And a share for the Goose, each thought, was better than an axe in your brain.

Back in the gullies they heard the roar.

"A share for the Goose."

Back in the gullies they started running again, started showing their teeth again. Back there they had stopped, with all their crazy hopes gone cold and sane. Hopes went wild again. On they came, swags lurching, barrows jolting.

"It's gold, it's gold, it's there, *it's there*."

> Sing Golden Goose,
> Sing Golden Goose,
> Sing Golden Goose, my hearty.

Custard was looking out to the plain.

It's a soldier, he thought, a real live soldier ridin' that horse. He's got a red coat on.

Come to save me, by gee, and about time.

He'll be having trouble, though, with this lot. Have you ever heard such a noise? They won't be likin' it, and there's a hundred of 'em, I reckon, all with bleary-lookin' eyes and whiskers around.

Ooooh, thought Custard. Look at that there! *Two* troopers! That's another coming in on his great big horse.

Wow.

And a *third* coming in on his great big horse!

Hooray. Hooray.

Three troopers coming this way, likety-split. One coming in from that way, and one coming in from over there, and look at the fella roaring up the middle with his long cloak flying.

"Shares for the Goose," they went on yelling, and had stones in their hands.

"They're goin' to stone me," Custard bellowed, and off he went, lurching and lunging through the ooze.

In came the trooper in the middle, black cloak flying, driving his horse at the mud, holding high a gun and firing a warning straight up that sounded like a crash from Heaven.

The strong horse reared, and almost every man saw the rider's hair fall loose as she drove the musket down into a holster and drew a pistol out and shrilled from the brink of the ooze, across the hush, "Come to me."

"It's the kid's mother!"

"My gawd, the Amazon."

Custard made a choking sound.

"In the name of the Law," a shout rang, "let the boy through or we'll send the dog in."

In the middle was the woman with her dog, and mounted troopers with pistols drawn were one to either side.

So suddenly it had happened.

"My mum," shrieked Custard. "She's come."

He went wading to her, yelling, and men round about wished to vanish into the ooze, to be out of the sight of the Law, as well as out of the memory of it.

"It's a hanging offence," roared the Law, "to take this boy from his mother and to be helping anyone who did it."

My mum loves me after all, thought Custard. My mum's come for me.

"Come on, Custard."

"I'm comin'."

Rebecca snapped a leash to White Dog's collar and started tying her horse to a tree.

"Come on, son, hurry out of there."

All at once it sounded a bit like *hurry, scurry, jump to it.* Came to Custard sounding like *hoe the row, fetch the bucket, chop the wood.* Shades of days gone by. Shades of Bella and shades of Seth.

A shadow in the ooze murmured, "Kill 'em, kill 'em, there's only two."

There were stirrings in the ooze.

Another said, "The kid can't go without his gold."

Custard stopped because he heard it. "Well, I'm goin' without it, aren't I? You took it away."

"We're givin' it back to you, kid."

The world was full of mysteries.

Someone near him said, "Take your gold."

"Don't you touch me," he squealed. "My mum's come for me. My mum can shoot the eye out of an eagle."

He went wading on towards her, dragging his feet up, squelching them down, and Rebecca was wading in, looking like something out of a battle between the Philistines and the Israelites.

That's my mum, thought Custard. She's really come.

A shout went rising up, "Don't leave your gold."

"My gold's gone," he said.

The noise became a wall and desperate men hid behind it, sheltered there in the noise, hid from the mad woman and the Law behind a generosity that became more and more reckless.

"Take your gold."

"Take your share."

Some threw gold, as if throwing stones, and others threw gold as if throwing it away.

> Sing the Goose who struck it, lads,
> Who found the El Dorado,
> Rich he'll be, but richer we
> Than Albert and the Queen, sir.

Rebecca came to Custard, a pistol in her right hand and White Dog straining in her left, and a stillness dropped as if the sheltering wall had burst and no one knew which way to turn.

White Dog leapt up, almost pulling Rebecca down, but Custard barely felt the weight for he was seeing her face grey and grimed and drawn, her eyes dark as if lights had gone out, her hands like bones, her clothing ripped as if shredded by knives.

"Are you well?" she said.

He thought it was a peculiar thing for her to say.

"I've got a cold," he said. "All this slish-sloshin' in the wet."

"Has anyone hurt you? That's what I'm asking." Her voice was strident.

Custard sighed, feeling a bit glum about it, wondering

what you had to count as hurt and what you counted otherwise.

Someone hit me with a shovel, he thought, and they've been draggin' me round by the neck for hours. They've been chuckin' stones an' all.

"If people have hurt you," Rebecca said, "point them out."

There were more movements in the ooze. There were murmurings again; hands went reaching for weapons again; and White Dog started growling, a disturbing sound.

"Not a man move," roared the Law from the edge of the ooze, "or we'll blow his head off."

"Don't you hear me?" Rebecca said to Custard.

He nodded.

"Well give me an answer. I can't believe nothing's happened to you."

Someone shot my Preacher Tom, Custard thought. Someone killed my Hector dead. But they all look the same, with their bleary-lookin' eyes and their whiskers around.

"Where are the hooligans who took you from home?" she demanded. "That man and his sons. That man and his gang. Where have they gone?"

Custard held out the cross in his hand.

"It's Preacher Tom's," he said, and suddenly cried, for he mourned for Preacher Tom and couldn't understand her harshness. "I can't find his grave any more. I can't find my Hector either. I can't find my friend Hector anywhere. He's lost and he's dead."

"You mean Hector *Button?*"

"My friend Hector's dead."

"What nonsense is this?"

"I don't want another dad. I can't stand the strain of losin' me dads."

He smeared at his tears with a muddy hand and something in her lightened and became a thread of joy confused with sadness.

What's been going on? Rebecca thought. He's out of another world, this child. He'll be the death of me. Has he been the death of that man?

Shyly, she placed her hand on his shoulder.

The grave, she thought, of that lovely man; is it here? Lost in this mud?

"Hector Button was your friend?"

"And I've lost my Preacher Tom."

She sighed to herself. But relief came to her and peace came to her. She had expected only to be using her gun. "Come on home, son."

Custard felt her hand there and it felt good, and he looked at White Dog and said, "I thought you were dead. This is White Dog," he explained, looking round. "If you get too close to my mum he eats you, and he don't spit out no bones neither."

"Doesn't," said Rebecca, "and *any* and *either.*"

"Doesn't," said Custard, "and any and either."

"The gold's the kid's share, lady," someone said. "For gawd's sake don't leave it lyin' there."

In the ooze, glistening stones were filming over with mud. Solid gold was disappearing like lumps of salt in the rain.

"Is that gold?" she said.

"You know it is, lady."

"Gold is for fools," she said.

"Little bits like that are," said Custard.

He went back towards the bluff, back to where the dragons and dinosaurs kept watch, and Jamie and Fred and Lou saw him and crept away as fast as they could crawl.

"Oh, lor," Jamie wailed. "She'll blast our heads off."

Rebecca waded after Custard. "Where are you taking me?"

He didn't answer her and didn't hear her.

Behind them, as they passed, astonished diggers started closing in to pick up the gold they had thrown.

"Not a man move," roared the Law.

They stopped, they froze, and leg by leg went on sinking into the ooze, as their gold went on sinking also, at least for a day.

"Not a man move," roared the Law at others coming in along the gullies, and they paused too, for unless you were quite mad the Law was larger than the troopers that you saw.

"Kill 'em, kill 'em, there's only two."

"Shut your mouth! They'll hear."

"Kill them."

Rebecca looked that rash man in the eye at thirty paces

and left him writhing with a bullet in his hand and with White Dog inches from his jaw.

The sound of the shot crashed against the bluff and Jamie and Fred and Lou almost died, and the shot crashed in Custard's head and sent him plunging to the mud.

"No man moves," Rebecca shouted. "Didn't you hear the trooper? So shoot me in the back, if that's the way you'd shoot a woman. *White Dog, let him be!*"

She pulled Custard up and passed through unharmed.

They stood at the edge where the ooze ended, and Custard's head still creaked from the crashing sound.

"Why did you come this way?" she said.

This way, he thought, is where I used the stick on the day the rain began. Over there the stick went arrowing into the ground like a spear or a sword and it rained and rained and rained. There's got to be a lump of gold over there as thick as my head and as long as my arm.

Then he thought of Jamie, and of Whistlin' Fred, and of Little Lou, and he didn't want White Dog getting their scent, and he didn't want his mum blasting their heads off. That would be a shame. And who'd be able to lift a lump of gold as big as a week of storm? Who'd ever get home with it alive? And, lor, if he spiked that lump of gold, it'd rain and rain and rain.

"I've forgotten why I came this way," he said to his mum. "Let's look for Little Horse instead. Preacher Tom gave him to me, he did. My very own horse, Little Horse is. Then we'll go home."

And as they went, the others came from the whole world round.

> Here we come from far and wide,
> From all around the earth, lads,
> Gold for me and gold for thee,
> And gold for Jack and Jill, sir.
>
> Gold for right and gold for wrong
> And gold for men to burn, lads,
> Gold to plug your aching teeth,
> And gold to buy the world, sir.
>
> Gorgeous gold for you and me,
> Oh gorgeous is the gold, lads,
> Gorgeous is the Golden Goose,
> The golden egg he laid, sir.

Books by Ivan Southall

MACMILLAN PUBLISHING CO., INC.
Josh
Head in the Clouds
Benson Boy
Matt and Jo
Hills End
Seventeen Seconds
Fly West
A Journey of Discovery
What About Tomorrow

ST. MARTIN'S PRESS, INC.
To the Wild Sky
The Curse of Cain
The Sword of Esau
Let the Balloon Go
Sly Old Wardrobe
Finn's Folly
Chinaman's Reef Is Ours

BRADBURY PRESS, INC.
Walk a Mile and Get Nowhere

GREENWILLOW BOOKS
Ash Road
King of the Sticks